WE ARE
THE ASHES,
WE ARE
THE FIRE

WE ARE THE ASHES, WE ARE THE FIRE

JOY McCULLOUGH

WITH ILLUMINATIONS BY
MAIA KOBABE

DUTTON BOOKS

DUTTON BOOKS

An imprint of Penguin Random House LLC, New York

Copyright © 2021 by Joy McCullough

Interior illustrations copyright © 2021 by Maia Kobabe

Penguin supports copyright. Copyright fuels creativity, encourages diverse voices, promotes free speech, and creates a vibrant culture. Thank you for buying an authorized edition of this book and for complying with copyright laws by not reproducing, scanning, or distributing any part of it in any form without permission. You are supporting writers and allowing Penguin to continue to publish books for every reader.

Dutton is a registered trademark of Penguin Random House LLC.

Visit us online at penguinrandomhouse.com

Library of Congress Cataloging-in-Publication Data is available.

Printed in the United States of America

ISBN 9780525556053

10 9 8 7 6 5 4 3 2 1

Design by Anna Booth

Text set in Garamond Premier Pro

For Jennifer, my sister

WE ARE
THE ASHES,
WE ARE
THE FIRE

BOYS

I'm
about
to tell you
a secret. you'd
like that, right?

secrets are
your favorite currency
                (power)
so come close
listen carefully:

                my body
                is not for you

                for your distraction
                your consumption
                your possession

I know you've been told
every second of your life
you're the center

I'd tell you I'm sorry
but that would be
another lie

if only you hadn't
skipped english lit
the day we learned
the center cannot hold

you think you'll hold forever

      all the power
      all the girls
      whatever body parts
      you want to grab

you'd make a joke
of the blood-dimmed tide
      (if you ever listened to ms. gregory)
but joke's on you
because just maybe
that blood flows from
all the girls you seek to possess
but one day we'll be loosed
and you'll be drowned

———

A poem wouldn't change anything, not even if I scrawled it on the walls of the boys' locker room at Fremont Middle School instead of into my notebook, while huddled in the back of the auditorium, choking on the fumes of Connor Olsen's vile body spray. Which would probably never wash out of my favorite hoodie.

Writing a poem was just something to do while the boys learned the fight choreography, the whole reason they'd signed up for the play, the chance to swing big swords. You'd think they'd have paid attention to the fight director, considering.

You'd be wrong.

I had to stay until the end in case I was needed, in case by some miracle the boys learned the choreography and there was still time to work on one of the few scenes I was in.

There wouldn't be time.

Finally I was released and Connor's body spray was no match for the crisp fall air as I walked north on Wallingford toward home. To the west, the Olympics stretched out along the peninsula; to the east, the Cascades separated Western Washington from the rest of the state.

I stopped at a light and the Eau de Boy caught up with me. Once I got home, I'd probably have to burn the hoodie. A ritual sacrifice to the goddess of middle school girls.

As if on cue, a pack of boys came barreling through, jostling me as they went. Did one of them grab my ass? *Don't be so sensitive, they were only brushing past.*

I ducked down an alley to avoid them at the next streetlight. The boy next door was a fairy tale. I'd known that since my mom told me about her first period. No big sister and Grandma didn't speak of such things, so Mom biked to the drugstore and used her birthday money to get everything she might need. She bought so many different products that on the way home everything toppled out of the bike basket and the boxes of pads and tampons spilled all over the street, right next to where a group of boys from her school were playing basketball.

She practically does a stand-up routine about it now. But it can't have been funny then, to scramble in the street retrieving everything she'd bought, everything she needed because of the body she was born with. What was she supposed to do? Leave it all? She'd spent her money. It would have been humiliating enough without those boys—they might as well be the same ones who just shoved past me on their way to the same basketball court—guffawing and shouting obnoxious things like it was all a hysterical joke.

Hysterical: from the Greek word for "uterus."

The refuge of the alley only lasted so long; I emerged where the boys' shouts at the basketball court still reached me, inescapable, but I wouldn't have to walk past the court. Instead, I was on the kind of Seattle street that's a mixture of hundred-year-old homes with inhabitants to match, mid-century bungalows, and the sleek, shiny-new structures of tech executives with Teslas parked in front.

I scowled at the SANDERS sign on a lawn as I passed. He lost the nomination ages ago, but the signs are still everywhere. Mom came home from that primary caucus so defeated—the Bernie Bros had won the day in the Fremont Elementary School cafeteria, and even if the rest of the country didn't agree, those guys would probably leave their signs out forever, unable to fathom that they hadn't gotten their way.

Papi couldn't vote, as a permanent resident, but he wore his LATINOS FOR HILLARY shirt and made molletes to comfort Mom after the caucus.

I couldn't understand why she was so upset. Washington State was Bernie country, maybe, but Clinton would get the nomination, with or without our state.

"It shouldn't have been such a struggle," Mom snapped at me. "And she hasn't won the presidency yet!"

Of course she would win. How could she not? She'd been working toward this since she graduated from Yale Law School. Before, probably. And her opponent was a complete buffoon with no qualifications and a whole list of sexual assault allegations against him.

We'd have our first female president soon. Which would open the floodgates for more women in politics. More women in charge.

And then, when the boys grabbed asses and sent dick pics, there'd be someone in power to make it stop.

———

Even the familiar smells of rising dough and Papi's marinara sauce were not enough to dull the edge of my fury as I burst into the house.

"I'm home, people!" I bellowed.

I didn't need to bellow. I could see at a glance the rest of my family, gathered in the kitchen where the ancient stove took the edge off the crisp air I'd brought in. They talked and laughed like the world wasn't a miserable cesspool of injustice.

"Always the picture of quiet refinement," Mom said with a grin as I dumped my bag and notebook on the ground, flung off the stinking hoodie, and slumped into a chair across from where Mom sat, hands wrapped around a chipped mug full of steaming tea, surrounded by student papers.

Grandpa used to bake in this kitchen too. Mom might have come home from the drugstore that day to the same instant-comfort smell of yeast and sugar and heat doing their chemical thing to transform into something completely new. It probably didn't make her forget those asshole boys, either.

"You want to talk about unrefined? Let me tell you about unrefined."

"I'm guessing we couldn't stop you." Nor stood at the counter, chopping garlic, her hair frizzing in the humidity of the kitchen. She paused to lift the lid on the sauce and steam clouded her glasses.

"Tell us the horrors of your day, canchita, of how you listened to the seas that love nothing but themselves," Papi said. "Pero ayuda while you're at it." He placed a cutting board, a knife, and two bell peppers on the table in front of me.

"Gabriela Mistral?" Nor asked as Mom's hand flew out to stop a damp green pepper from rolling onto a freshman English composition.

"Así es," Papi said, hurrying back to the stove to stir the sauce. More steam. "Escuchando mares que no aman sino a sí mismos."

"Middle school boys," I said, ignoring the poetry lesson and pointing with the knife for emphasis, "are unrefined. Ugh, I cannot wait for high school."

Nor laughed. "High school boys are worse."

"Impossible."

"They're at least not any better." Nor scooped the chopped garlic into her palm and moved to drop it in the sauce, our father countering her as he reached for the oregano on the windowsill, a perfectly choreographed dance in our tiny kitchen.

"Fine then, college," I said, making slow, careful slices into the peppers on the ancient wooden cutting board my uncle made in woodshop a million years ago. There's a scorch mark where Mom set a too-hot pan when she was my age, but Grandma didn't throw it out. I didn't have my sister's knife skills—or any of her kitchen skills, really. It all took so much time and care, the perfect measurements, exact right temperatures. "Bring on the college men!"

Mom looked up from her grading in alarm.

"Not yet, obviously. Just like, today was supposed to be fight choreography? And Alex and Connor were being such boys!"

"Pero what a lazy description," Papi said as he pulled the pizza dough from the bowl and began to shape it. "Was their behavior directly related to their anatomy?"

I rolled my eyes.

He continued. "I'm sure you don't want to hear my lecture on the power of specific word choice—"

"I really don't."

"I love that lecture," Mom said, making moony eyes across the kitchen at him.

"They were being revolting and immature and super disrespectful of the fight choreographer, who was completely amazing."

"Mucho más específico," Papi crowed, making a failed attempt to toss the crust, which he speared with his hand on its descent.

"She's a student from Cornish—"

"Who?" Mom said.

"The fight choreographer! The sequence looked so cool when she was doing it, but they weren't even listening, they were just screwing around."

"How are those peppers coming?"

I glanced at the cutting board. I'd only cut a few slices before I started venting about rehearsal. Between my righteous anger and the alchemy in the kitchen, my flannel was too much. I shrugged it off and kept cutting. "If I got to do any fighting, it would be amazing. But all I do is sit there, cheering on my man."

"I've always hated the Arthurian legends." Mom began to clear the table of her freshman compositions. "Brave knights and fair maidens." She snorted. "Only the compliant women are good, and the women with any power at all are evil. Don't get me started on the vilification of women's sexuality."

"We won't," Nor and I responded in unison, then exchanged a glance. I giggled and Nor quickly turned away to stifle her laugh in the refrigerator.

"But it was medieval times," I said. "That's what the gender roles were then. It's different now. Or it would be if middle school boys weren't stupid."

"Canchita," Papi said, coming around the counter to rescue the peppers. He placed a warm, heavy hand on my shoulder. "It is a truth universally acknowledged that middle school boys son tontos. Estoy seguro que you will make the most of your role in the play, even if you must play a compliant woman. Consider it an acting challenge you will master with verve."

As he turned back to the counter, Nor tossed the pizza crust in the air, catching it perfectly.

"Show-off." Papi shook his head. "When are you going to open a Michelin-star restaurant and make us all rich?"

"Em can make us rich," she said with a faint smile. "Marine biologists don't make that much money."

Always with the marine biology. Nor had been focused on that forever. I, on the other hand, had no goal beyond washing the smell of middle school boy off my body. Connor wouldn't listen during fight choreography, but he had no problem following instructions when the director told King Arthur to hold Guinevere close.

"Do I have time for a shower before the pizza's ready?"

"If you make it quick," Nor said.

I headed from the room.

"Boots, backpack, journal, room," Mom called after me.

I doubled back, grabbed the stuff I dropped earlier, and left my parents grilling Nor on how she liked the new advisor for the high school paper.

I didn't care what Nor said. High school had to be better than middle school. Especially the boys.

CHAPTER ONE

"You can't react." Mom smooths her hair for the forty-seventh time since we parked in the public garage a block away from the courthouse. Now we sit in the freezing car. Waiting. "No matter what. All the cameras—"

"I know."

"Don't snap at your mother, Marianne."

I watch the slice of Papi's face in the rearview mirror. The fresh gray at his temples, the new lines around his eyes. *Weary* would be a specific word choice.

They're so afraid, my larger-than-life parents. Shrinking into themselves for nearly a year, layering on armor that doesn't even protect them. Retreating when they should have been on the front lines. With me.

My fury begins to unfurl, deep down. If I stay trapped in their inaction, it will spill out, blazing hot, and scorch them until their skin blisters, the seats of this ancient car melt, the whole thing burns down.

"I have to stretch my legs."

I bolt from the car before they can object.

They would object. They want to keep me close, muzzle me, *don't write your columns about the case, Marianne, don't be so outspoken, Em, don't, don't, don't.*

Outside the car, I'm free of their crushing inaction but I'm boxed in by the dark, low ceilings of the parking garage, the stench of furtive smoke breaks, urine, and gasoline seeped into concrete that'll never be washed clean.

I walk toward the hazy light of the exit to the street. Every step I take away from the car, I know my mom is fretting. We're supposed to wait for Layla! Walk in together. United front!

But the slick sidewalk grounds me, the damp air, the concrete and steel fading into skies that are yet another shade of gray. This is my Seattle. I dig a dollar out of my pocket and hand it to the guy huddled in the opposite corner of the parking garage entrance.

Mom can still see me from the car. And I can see the courthouse down the block. It was imposing at first. Now, after so many months, I yawn at the building. The way my sister's tabby always yawned his ambivalence about human existence. Until he got hit by a car, at which point he was probably less ambivalent.

Across the street, a guy immersed in his phone looks up, leers. Does he recognize me from the trial coverage? Or is he a dime-a-dozen dirtbag?

I hold his gaze until he looks away.

Dirtbag, then. The trial never looks away.

Even after it's over—so soon, it will be over—its gaze will linger.

A car pulls into the garage and I catch a glimpse of Layla's hijab, bright orange in the dull beige of her ancient station wagon. Nor pulls in right behind Layla, as though the victim advocate took her job so seriously she escorted my sister all the way from campus. Really, we're all here at the same time by horrible circumstance.

Papi climbs out of our car and heads around to open Mom's door like he always does, but she bursts out on her own.

"Good morning." Layla's voice echoes in the parking garage and I flinch at the slam of her car door. "How are we doing?"

Papi gives her a tight smile and nod, but Mom can't rip her eyes off my sister's car. She's fighting every instinct she has to race over, throw open Nor's door, and yank her out into her arms. I know, because I'm doing the same thing.

"We're okay," I say. "How are you?"

Layla gives her familiar smile, the one we've seen for months. It manages to be warm and supportive, while never dismissing the reason she's in our lives. "One of my neighbor's new chickens has turned out to be a rooster," she says. "But aside from that I can't complain."

When this is all over, I'll send Layla a thank-you for all the time she spent answering my questions about legal procedures, and what all the various charges meant. The difference between "indecent liberties" and "assault with sexual motivation." If I could make sure my high school paper got it right, the *Seattle Times* reporters could have spent a bit more time critiquing how our system works and less time weeping over the lost potential of Craig Lawrence's future.

Nor still doesn't get out of the car. My parents wanted to pick her up, arrive together. But they didn't insist when she said she'd drive herself. *She needs to feel like she's in control,* Mom said, like we haven't all read the same books and websites about supporting survivors.

Mom starts toward Nor's car, but Layla places a gentle hand on her arm. "Give her a minute?"

Layla's as badass as they come but she doesn't need to talk like an alpha male to get my mom to listen. I could throat-punch every armchair pundit who criticized Nor's uptalk in the one interview she gave—and the defense attorney for defining her speech patterns as "hesitant."

When Nor finally emerges, though, Mom doesn't hold herself back. Layla doesn't stop her—she's Nor's advocate, not her bodyguard. *She doesn't like to be touched anymore,* I want to scream as Mom fusses over Elinor's everything. Perfect collar, perfect hair, perfect cheeks. If everything looks perfect, maybe we won't shatter into a million irretrievable pieces.

I pull my hair out of its ponytail, let the wind rip through it. My lungs seize in the unusually cold air and I breathe deep to spite it.

In the midst of Mom's hovering, Nor catches my eye. I tell myself she's going to roll her eyes any second. *Classic Mom, right?* We're going to share a moment like always, Em and Nor, Nor and Em, they basically share a brain.

But before the moment can flicker into a flame, Layla clears her throat. "All right. Everybody ready?" A flame never stood a chance in this wind anyway.

We move as a group, a funeral procession. Layla puts herself between us and the scrum of reporters as we approach the courthouse steps, but she's small, no match for a dozen cameras. I glare defiantly, give them something to photograph while Elinor looks demurely down. They might think we're allies because I wanted this story covered, I fed them tips, but being Twitter mutuals doesn't give them a right to treat my sister like a Hollywood starlet with a wardrobe malfunction.

Though the reporters are kept outside, the probing eyes, the pointing never ends. Through security, up the stairs, more glares, more scrutiny, better suited to someone headed for the defense table, accused of a terrible crime, but instead, once inside the courtroom Layla leads us to the seats behind the prosecutor's table.

Once upon a time, Nor and I sat together through every family movie, school assembly, wedding, funeral, holiday dinner. But now my parents flank my sister, leaving me to the side. It's not about me. I get it. But also I want to crash through their miserable attempt at a fortress, take Nor's hand, and remind her that I'm the one who's never wavered, never given up belief that she would have justice.

The assistant district attorney appears in front of us, gives me an encouraging nod, then turns to Elinor and my parents, murmuring softly. She's young, newly appointed, passionate. She's made an excellent case. When she almost took an absurd plea deal—only six months for violent rape with a witness?—she listened when I sent her the *Oracle* piece I wrote about the Jacob Anderson case. She considered the Twitter attention around the article and held out for actual justice.

Our case couldn't have gone better, really. In a brutal, horrific, gut-splattering way.

The only thing that remains is for the jury to deliver their verdict, the judge to render his sentence. For Craig Lawrence to go to prison for the rest of time.

The jury files in. I study their faces. The single mom who works double shifts as a nurse to stay afloat. She's tough, hardened by the horrors she's seen in the ER. The high school dropout who made it big with a tech start-up. He drives a Tesla and brews his own IPAs. The kindergarten teacher who's so burned out that she's seen these weeks on the jury as a vacation. The notes she's constantly jotting down are occasionally about the trial, but mostly they're for the sci-fi trilogy she's writing.

These aren't their real identities, their actual stories. These are fantasies I dreamed up when the trial devolved into hours of analyzing and comparing fiber samples, or when I couldn't bear to hear Craig Lawrence's smug, lying voice anymore. Then I'd stare at these people who held Nor's fate—all our fates—in their hands and try to figure out who they were and how their experiences—imagined though they were—might lead them to judge the monster on trial.

The final moments when we're waiting for everyone to get settled, the jury forewoman to stand, to finally spit out what's on the folded piece of paper in her bony fingers, are agonizing.

Was I wrong? Was it all for nothing? I can't bear to lean over and look at Nor's face. We've come all this way and I'm abandoning her now, but her hope will crush me as much as her defeat.

Because I realize in a flash that this could go either way. The clear evidence, witnesses, Nor's squeaky-clean image . . . it's not always enough. I've been hopeful, but not stupid.

"Has the jury reached a unanimous verdict?" the judge asks.

"We have." The forewoman's voice shakes, like it's her life on the line.

The clerk retrieves the paper from the woman and delivers it to the judge. He reads. His brow furrows. There's no way to guess what it means. The clerk's walk back to the forewoman stretches out for a millennium.

The forewoman takes the paper and draws in her breath. The courtroom holds the breath with her.

"On the count of unlawful imprisonment," she reads.

At the defense table, Craig Lawrence gives the tiniest shake of his head, like it's so absurd. It's not imprisonment to take a drunk girl into an alley.

"We find the defendant guilty."

Relief all around me. But that's the least of the charges. My breath is still shallow.

"On the count of indecent liberties," she reads.

Flashback to Tyler Jacobsen in the cafeteria, laughing and shouting that he was going to take some indecent liberties right before grinding on Patrice Kuan.

"We find the defendant guilty."

Voices murmur throughout the gallery.

"On the count of assault in the second degree with sexual motivation," she reads, her voice stumbling over the word *sexual*.

Craig's lawyer has a comforting arm around his shoulder. The men in suits behind him are already on their phones, mobilizing their brotherhood for whatever comes next. The papers will write with pity about the defendant's lack of weeping family, but who needs family when you've got the patriarchy in your corner?

"We find the defendant guilty."

My mother starts to sob. It's good. But there's still one more charge to go.

"On the count of second-degree rape," she reads.

The plea deal would have dropped this count. He'd have served a few months for the assault charge. But this is the one that can put him away for life.

"We find the defendant guilty."

Nor sits silent, stunned, as the courtroom explodes around her. I search her face for a reaction. It's not like I expected her to dance around the end zone. This doesn't change what happened to her, this monstrous cloud that will follow her forever—not only the brutal attack, but also the trial, the reporters, the dissection of every aspect of her life.

Get photographed with a red Solo cup in your hand? Noted.

Dress up as "sexy" Amelia Earhart for Halloween? Noted.

Have an immigrant father? Noted.

Both my parents are sobbing now. The urge to smack them startles me. This is a good thing. But I tried to tell them. They didn't believe me.

Idealistic Marianne, things don't always turn out the way you hope, it doesn't matter how cut and dried the case, how many survivors you profile in your high school paper—none of that is going to change our justice system . . .

I'm relieved, of course. But now I need the sentence. Everyone in this courtroom knew that smug fucker was guilty. The question is, how is he going to pay?

———

Nor comes home with us, instead of returning to her dorm. We've been begging her to come, but she's insisted on staying on campus, even through the summer, insisted she wouldn't let him take her college experience too.

But the sentence won't come for weeks. Maybe months. Now that she's won, she wants to be home.

That's wrong—this was no victory.

The first several times Nor's phone buzzes, I think it must be her friends. But her brow pinches together a little each time she scans the screen until she turns her phone off and shoves it under the couch cushion. She rolls her neck, working out those ever-present aches and pains.

"Do you want my heating pad?" I ask.

"Too hot."

I never use mine. I only have it because it was in the period kit Mom gave me when I was twelve. Since that night, Nor uses heating pads, rice bags, hot water bottles—not that any of them help her much.

Mom and Papi sing in the kitchen. This super-old Nat King Cole song in Spanish, which my dad sings with a terrible-on-purpose accent. It's an inside joke. They're deliriously happy.

Irritation flashes across Nor's face and I know the next second she'll be on her feet and headed to her room.

"Want to watch something? You can pick."

She shrugs. But she stays.

While she scrolls through the options, I don't say, *You were so brave, Nor.* I don't say, *I was terrified that I'd pushed you into the whole circus of a trial and then it would be for nothing.* I don't say, *I know it doesn't change anything of what happened to you but that asshole's never going to hurt another girl and I've never been prouder you're my sister.*

Instead I roll my eyes at the dusty old period drama she chooses for the zillionth time, like an heirloom quilt so worn the pattern's barely visible, but as warm as ever. "Really?" I say. "Again?"

And she says what I know she will, what she always says: "Mr. Darcy forever, little sister."

CHAPTER TWO

The first few days after the verdict, I make good use of Megan Hart's standard advice for dealing with trolls: Mock, block, and roll. If anyone knows how to deal with wounded MRAs on the internet, it's Megan, with her years of outspoken advocacy.

The first time Megan retweeted one of my *Oracle* profiles, I screamed so loud Papi came running. I shoved my phone in his face and he screamed too. The only way the moment could have been more perfect is if he had been wearing his BRAZEN HUSSY T-shirt from Megan's first book tour.

Hussy: a once-neutral term that meant "female head of the household."

Ms. Lim didn't believe me at first when I said it was a good thing the *Oracle* website crashed. But I was right. That one retweet brought in a ton more traffic, which equaled ad dollars for the paper. More important, it persuaded Ms. Lim to let me keep writing the profiles of survivors denied justice. Our little compromise when she told me I couldn't write about my own sister's case.

When I got to introduce Megan at the Seattle Women for Choice rally, Ms. Lim was in the front row, wearing a BRAZEN HUSSY T-shirt of her own. My journalism advisor disagrees with Megan on one thing—she tells me to ignore haters in the comments. But Twitter is not journalism and trolls deserve to be mocked. And then forgotten.

Most of the people in my mentions are celebrating anyway, heralding the sweep of guilty charges as a shift in our rape culture. Even the old boys clubs of Greeks and jocks rallying bail money and legal fees for poor, disadvantaged Craig Lawrence weren't enough to keep him from facing justice.

After the first week, though, my mentions go quiet. The feminist accounts move on to organizing a march for reproductive rights and raising funds for the medical bills of a rape victim at Ohio State. Journalism accounts are focused on a missing reporter in Syria. I search familiar Husky hashtags and find almost nothing related to our case.

It's almost like everyone has moved on, but then I get an email from Kylie, whose *Oracle* profile was the first one Megan Hart retweeted. The one that crashed our server.

Dear Marianne,

I heard about the verdict and I wanted to reach out. First, to explain why I ghosted you there for a few months. You did a really good job with the piece. But I never expected an article in a high school paper to get so much attention. So even though it was anonymous, I felt kind of exposed. Afraid my attacker would see it and know it was me. My girlfriend read the supportive comments to me, though, and it really helped so much to see all those people believing me. Thank you for that.

Anyway, I was so glad to see the guilty verdict in your sister's case. I wish we could all get that justice, but seeing it when it happens gives me hope. Your sister is lucky to have your support. I hope you're doing well and I wish you all the best in your writing and your advocacy.

Sincerely,
Kylie Hancock

"Good news?" Mom's in my doorway, shivering in Papi's robe.

"Yeah, one of my profile subjects wrote. Really grateful."

She nods like she hasn't even heard me. "Aren't you freezing? I'm freezing."

"Have we not figured out the deal with the thermostat? I'm wearing layers." I tug on my sweats to show her the leggings underneath. "She had her girlfriend read her the positive comments on my article and she was really encouraged."

"Hmm." Mom pulls the robe tighter. "Papi and I are stumped. I called Uncle Joel. He's going to try to swing by and look at it. I'm making chai. Do you want some?"

"Yeah, thanks." I bite back my irritation.

But then Mom pauses as she heads back to the kitchen. "You aren't going to keep writing those profiles now, are you? Now that it's over?"

"What?"

"Never mind."

It's not over. Not for Nor, who flinches at any sudden noise, who pops ibuprofen like the worst candy ever to ease her endless pain. Not for Papi, who dies a little every time Nor doesn't feel like cooking, whose face darkens at the sight of Husky gear. It's not over for me.

Before my irritation can grow into something bigger, I've got a new message in my inbox. From Megan Hart.

Hey, Em,

Greetings from Olympia, where I am banging down doors, trying to get a meeting about a statewide expansion of Seattle's all-gender bathroom ordinance. Wish me luck.

I saw the verdict. It's a good step. I just want to warn you not to count your chickens, or whatever the saying is. Judges have a way of taking would-be chicks and making them into a tasty omelet. This metaphor has gotten away from me. Point is, he's guilty: HELL YES HE IS. But be prepared for all outcomes with the sentencing, okay?

Burn it all down,
MH

I'm so distracted that night, between my mom's comments and Megan's message, that I can barely enjoy Uncle Joel's visit. He brings pizza, fixes the thermostat, teases Mom mercilessly while clearly adoring his little sister. But if he'd been there when Mom spilled tampons all over the street, would he have helped her? Or would he have laughed with the rest of the boys?

"Keep smashing the patriarchy, Lois Lane," he says by way of goodbye as he leaves.

I'm pretty sure he would have laughed.

———

The next morning I dig through my closet—Gryffindor robe, way-too-small tap shoes, the misshapen poncho Nor made when she first learned to knit—until I find it. The deep blue Moleskine Papi gave me when I graduated from sixth grade.

"For poetry?" I'd asked. He'd carried a similar leather-bound notebook in his back pocket for as long as I could remember, jotting down scraps of verse as they came to him.

"Para lo que sea, canchita."

For whatever I wanted.

It was my constant companion for a year. I'm sure the poetry is terrible; I'm not looking back to see. But it gave me a place to dump all my anger and confusion and emotion before it bubbled over and I got called dramatic.

I'd probably have filled it up and moved on to another except that during tech week of *The Knights of the Round Table*, Dustin Smalley snuck into the girls' dressing room and stole it. I'd been made fight captain and the boys didn't take kindly to me bossing them around.

Bossy: used to describe girls who show leadership skills.

So he stole the notebook. Took pictures of the most emotional, dramatic pages. Posted them all over.

When Papi asked where my Moleskine was, I shrugged and told him I'd outgrown it. The hurt on his face killed me, but it was better than telling him the truth. Plus I wasn't going to stop writing. I just wouldn't write anything that could hurt me.

I got it back, but I buried it in my closet. I let Dustin Smalley and Connor Olsen and all those small, insecure boys take poetry from me.

I'm done letting boys take anything from me.

CHAPTER THREE

We return to the courtroom for the sentencing two months after hearing the verdict. Time has become an unreliable narrator, stretching and compressing at will, with no regard for a victim's family living perpetually on the edge of what might come next.

Layla, ever present, joins us on our familiar, uncomfortable seats from the trial. She reminds us of what's to come: There will be statements from the lawyers, from Craig and his supporters.

Nor could give a victim impact statement—stand there in front of not only her rapist, but the lawyers who tore her apart, the public who judged her every decision as though she had a choice in what mattered, and live it all again.

Some survivors do. One hundred and fifty-six gymnasts gave statements directly to the team doctor who violated them. *Little girls don't stay little forever. They grow into strong women that destroy your world.*

Chanel Miller made a victim impact statement that went viral, was translated into other languages, read on the House floor. *Every minute of every day, you are powerful and nobody can take that away from you. To girls everywhere, I am with you.*

But Nor's elected not to let this courtroom have another moment of her pain; she's had enough of her every word dissected on the witness stand, her every hesitation, inflection, tone. Layla assured her it was her choice. It wasn't likely to change anything anyway. The judge will have already decided the sentence when he walks in the room.

It's so pointless, one last chance for everyone to play their parts.

The defense bemoans the loss of potential for this bright young man on academic scholarship who only wanted to fit in with the football players and fraternity brothers.

The prosecutor focuses on the brutality of the crime, Nor's injuries, the reliable (translation: cis-male) witness to her inability to consent, the precedent a light sentence would set.

Craig himself dares to glance at Nor as he tells the courtroom he's really sorry if Nor regretted the time they spent together. Aw shucks, golly gee, he even manages a blush when he says he maybe came on a little strong because he was nervous, he'd never been with such a pretty girl.

Been with.

I take Nor's hand. It's cold and shaking. I want to throw my body in front of hers, shield her. Maybe I imagine it, but behind the cocksure grin there's a flicker of fear. He's a monster, absolutely, but he's still uncertain how this is going to play out. The finest lawyers patriarchy can buy couldn't keep him from a guilty verdict. Who's to say how long he'll rot in prison?

When all attention turns to the judge, I feel a swell of something unfamiliar. Patriotism? After so many months of railing against our system, profiling survivors failed by police and juries and lawyers and judges, and even their parents and teachers and friends, I'm suddenly proud of our justice system. Riding a wave at its absolute peak. Not many victims like Nor see justice, but she will.

"All right then," he says gruffly, shuffling papers before him. "I've had a great deal to think about since our jury rendered its verdict. I'd like to thank those men and women for doing their job, and now, my role is to follow the guidelines our system of criminal justice sets out for the Court in sentencing decisions.

"Before I get to the sentence, I want to recognize that Elinor's life has been devastated by these events—not only the incidents that happened, but also the media attention given to this case, which compounds the difficulties that participants in the criminal process face. So I acknowledge that devastation.

"As I consider Mr. Lawrence's sentence, I have had to ask myself, consistent with the Rules of Court: Will state prison for the defendant alter this devastation? Is incarceration the right answer for his lapse in judgment?"

My patriotism slips. The wave is breaking.

He drones on, mentioning specific penal codes and legal intoxication levels, credibility of witnesses, mitigating factors, moral culpability and vulnerability of the victim, the lack of prior criminal record, youth of the offender, and character letters.

Nobody cares what Craig Lawrence's Sunday School teacher thinks he's capable of. The judge might wish he could protect Lawrence, but a jury of his peers saw differently.

"Now we come to the most compelling factor in my opinion: the adverse collateral consequences on the defendant's life resulting from these specific charges. And those are severe. With respect to the media attention that's been given to the case, it has not only impacted the accuser in this case, but also Mr. Lawrence."

Of course the wave breaks. They always do.

"With regards to remorse, Mr. Lawrence, in his state of intoxication, saw the events in a certain way. If he were to, for the benefit of a lighter sentence or to pacify the Court, state otherwise, which I'm sure defendants do all the time, he really would be not honest. So I take him at his word that, subjectively, that's his version of events, and I want to applaud his honesty."

The wave crashes onto the rocks below.

"The jury, obviously, found it not to be the sequence of events. Our criminal justice system relies on juries to evaluate facts and to come to very difficult decisions about specific factual incidents. But given the various factors I've outlined here, I feel it is unclear that Ms. Morales was incapacitated to a degree that would support second-degree rape or indecent liberties, or the sexual motivation enhancement to the assault charge. Which leaves second-degree assault and unlawful imprisonment, which, for the reasons I have explained, I believe warrant a downward departure from the SRA guidelines. Therefore I am sentencing Mr. Lawrence to time served."

Someone hits pause on the courtroom drama that is our life. There's a suspended breath around me as dots are connected:

Downward departure.
Lapse in judgment.
Applaud his honesty.
Adverse collateral consequences.
Time served.

The lawyers understand what the judge has said, they must. Next to me, Layla has gone rigid. The prosecutor lets out the slightest huff of frustration. But if everyone else understood, they'd be storming the bench. Wouldn't they? I'm not sure even Nor realizes Craig will walk out of here without prison time. I can't be the one to tell her.

The judge's gavel comes down and the pause is released.

At the defense table, men in suits clap Craig on the shoulder. Behind us, the people in the gallery begin to buzz. This time my parents don't weep. They sit, frozen, completely useless to Nor. Her hands shake, grasping vaguely in front of her, like she might find something to hold on to in the wreckage.

It takes me half a second too long and my face flushes with shame, but then I'm crouching in front of her, taking those grasping hands, being her lifeboat.

"Nor," I say, that one syllable pouring out like a waterfall. I was the one who pushed her into this I was the one who stopped the plea deal I was the one—

"Don't," she says, and jerks her hands back.

A tidal wave of movement carries us out of the courthouse, through the hall, down the stairs, and into an alcove near the front doors where Layla and the lawyers say words, presumably words, but mostly their mouths are moving and sound is coming out, but nothing means anything anymore.

None of it mattered, none of what I did this last year, all those profile pieces, all the Twitter followers, Megan Hart's retweets.

The dragon came and I fought valiantly, and right when it seemed like the fair maiden would be saved and all the village with her, he let out one dying gasp of fire and it was enough to burn us all to ash.

Nor's hands still shake, but her eyes are as blank as they were that night.

I've been so naive.

Layla nudges my arm, guides us to the front doors, the courthouse steps, into the flashing cameras, shouted questions.

It's all a mess of ash and guilt and smoke and ruins. I pull away from Layla and shove through the reporters. My knees slam into the concrete as I drop to the ground, the weight of every camera turned on me. Fingers in the dirt of the courthouse landscaping, lives destroyed here but at least it's pretty, I empty myself of everything I didn't already give these vultures.

Let them photograph that.

"Miss Morales," says a reporter, shoving a camera in my face as I wipe a string of bile from my cheek. "How do you feel about the sentence?"

Staring straight into the camera, I speak loud and clear. "I feel"—I calmly get to my feet—"like learning how to use a fucking sword."

CHAPTER FOUR

They play the clip over and over. Analyze my mental health, delve into a possible family history of violence, Papi's childhood in the most gang-ridden area of Guatemala City. Perhaps the defense's case held water: The accuser consented and simply liked it rough. If the father comes from violence and the younger sister has a taste for it, why not Elinor Morales as well?

Spoiler alert: Twitter bros are seriously into the idea of women liking it rough. Some of the feminist accounts turn on me too. *We can't play into the notion of feminists as violent man-haters.*

Megan Hart is silent.

I feel like learning how to use a fucking sword.

My mother sobs; Papi shuts himself in their room. Probably writing agonized poetry, like words are going to save us now. I already wrote the words. Specific words. They were never going to save us.

I feel like learning how to use a fucking sword.

And Elinor, Elinor packs to go back to school, to a campus still mourning the unjust conviction of their adopted darling or celebrating the dismissal of the charges that mattered most. The championed cause of generations of SAE brothers and football fans won't see a day of jail. And still the university campus is pissed by the "distraction" to the Husky program. Never mind that football isn't even in season.

I want to insist the DA remand the case for resentencing.

I want to mount a campaign against the judge's reelection.

But: "Please, Em," Nor whispers in my ear before she leaves for her dorm, "don't cause any more trouble."

Em is trouble.

That's what everyone's said from the time I was old enough to use my voice, my enormous voice, so loud when Elinor's was so not. Always talking, people marveled, until I got too old for that to be adorable, which wasn't nearly long enough.

Then I was brash, I was brazen, I was bossy.

I wore bossy like armor, polished it in the rare moments I removed it. Let them call me bossy. I was still in charge of every game, every skit, every revolution. I hit the boys, and it wasn't because I liked them.

But Elinor, she's sugar and spice, that's what they all say, and I don't begrudge my sister the adoration, either. I polished my sword until it gleamed because Nor is a princess and a dragon would come soon enough, because that's the way of things, and my brash, pushy self would be there to boss it back where it came from.

The dragon came.

My sword wasn't enough.

CHAPTER FIVE

The newspaper staff goes to Roxy's Diner to celebrate the last day of school, but I make an excuse. They'll constantly be checking if I'm okay like they have since the sentencing and of course I'm not okay but I'll end up assuring them that I am. Anyway, they'll spend the rest of the time talking about Summer Intensive in Denver.

When Ms. Lim first told me I couldn't go, and worse, that I couldn't be editor of the paper next year, I was pissed. I'm over it now. There are too many other things to be furious about.

It was worth posting my unauthorized editorial on the *Oracle* website. Especially since Summer Intensive will be a nonstop parade of instructors telling high school journalists they can change the world through the power of words.

They can't.

I push out the double doors and into the June gloom. Too many people crowd under the overhang at the bus stop, so I stand in the drizzle and ignore my phone when it buzzes.

It won't be Nor.

Without the scheduled six-week journalism program, the summer stretches out before me, vast and open in a way that feels more oppressive than free. It can't be worse than last summer, though, when the investigation was underway and Husky fans were pissed about the preseason off-field distraction.

Something bumps my shoulder and I stumble into the old woman next to me.

"I'm sorry!" I reach out to steady the woman, who smiles graciously but also mutters, "Puro puerco," as she moves away.

The first time I heard that I thought my tío Gallo was calling me a pig, as in fat, and Papi had to explain that the expression means clumsy, because pigs always walk around with their noses to the ground.

"God, Summer, rude!" says a voice behind me. And then, "I'm sorry for my friend's uncouth behavior."

Jess from my English class stands with their shadow, a girl named Summer with a permanent scowl. I'm not sure I've ever seen her smile. Maybe when she goes to college, she'll change her name to something that suits her more. Like Astrid. Or Zelda. Like college is this big chance for reinvention.

"It's not real." Jess nods at the suit of armor in Summer's arms, which is what shoved me into the old woman. As though I thought it was an actual medieval relic. "Just foam. You're on the paper, right?"

The bus pulls up. "No," I say. "I'm not."

I get on the bus, slouch into a seat next to a middle-aged woman absorbed in her book. She's the sort who probably followed the trial obsessively, knitting pink hats while watching the news. But there aren't many seats open, and the woman doesn't look at my face.

Jess and Summer get on and I avoid their eyes as they pass.

"If you want to joust, you'll have to get real armor," Jess says, their voice carrying two rows up and across the aisle.

"I don't want to joust with those assholes," Summer says. "I want to run my longsword through their guts."

Jess laughs. "Look at you, all Lady Snowblood."

Summer gasps. "Do not associate me with that male-fantasy garbage!"

"Fine then. You're . . . Marguerite de Bressieux."

They say it with this exaggerated French accent, and Summer laughs at the reference. Could be a feminist icon or a regular on the Ren Faire circuit for all I know. I've been so absorbed in all things legal justice for the last year and a half that I'm waking from a coma, totally disoriented to the world of normal teenagers.

They speak a completely different language. A language of happy lives with happy friends and happy hobbies. I shove earbuds in and drown their unbearable happiness in white noise.

CHAPTER SIX

My father is a monster. He knows I want to hole myself up in my room, and so he devotes his afternoon to making jocón, the smells of which waft down the hall and under the crack in my door. All afternoon, chicken simmers in tomatillos and cilantro and toasted pumpkin seeds.

I'm pissed. But also hungry.

In the kitchen, he stands at the stove, slapping tortilla dough between his palms. He holds up a lopsided oval and grins. It takes him about ten times longer to make each tortilla than the women in Guatemala who stand at the comals all day, babies strapped to their backs, endlessly producing the staple food of their communities. Growing up, Papi could run to any corner at mealtimes and pay pennies for a stack of fresh, piping-hot tortillas.

"Nice one." I slide onto a barstool, flip through the junk mail. "Very tortilla-adjacent."

"Want to try?" He offers a ball of dough across the counter.

I take it, remembering the first time I tried to shape the dough in my uncle's kitchen. Tío Gallo laughed at my attempt but told me the shape didn't matter; a wonky oval would scoop up the beans just as well as a perfect circle.

The masa feels like Play-Doh between my fingers, but weightier. The Mayan gods fashioned people out of cornmeal after their first attempts failed; mud and wood did not a human race create. Even the gods make mistakes.

"Whoa, whoa, you've got to be gentle with the masa." Papi cringes at the pulverized mess between my fingers. "¿Te acuerdas? One hand twists, while the other lightly—"

"I don't want to tortillear."

He sighs, takes the mess of dough back. "Then make the salad, canchita. Have you given any more thought to what you're going to do with your summer?"

Translation: Have you applied for any of the ninety-three jobs I've suggested?

"Working on it." I squeeze around him in our tiny kitchen to pull the salad things from the fridge. "Where's Mom? I thought she wasn't teaching any evening classes this semester."

"She's covering an American Lit class. Margaret's baby came earlier than expected."

My brain snags on Margaret and I'm back on the bus, just for a second. All the things I've missed.

But Margaret is not Marguerite—she's Mom's office mate. I glance at the calendar. I thought her baby wasn't due until mid-July. But I don't really know what's early and what's too early, with babies. What's nerve-racking and what's world-ending. The line seems scary thin.

All the lines are scary thin, turns out.

"The receptionist job is still open at the gym, but Carlos can't hold it for long," Papi says.

I nod. It would be pretty mind-numbing swiping hard-bodies into a gym all summer, but mind-numbing might not be a bad thing. "Yeah, I'll call him."

"Marianne," Papi begins, the rare utterance of my actual name from his lips, the *r* tripping like a pebble over water. But then his phone rings. He lunges, the same way I used to lunge, back when I thought Nor might call. Which she won't.

"Lo siento," Papi says when he gets off the phone. "Me tengo que ir. Burst pipe in Belltown." He's already in emergency mode, off to save the hipsters of Seattle from clogged drains and spilled sewage. "The jocón is ready, and there should be enough tortillas already made."

"I'm fine, Papi. Go."

Then it's just me. And Chester, who comes padding into the kitchen as soon as Papi's gone. He knows I won't order him out, even if he gets underfoot. In fact, odds are good I'll take two bites, then set my bowl on the ground for the galumphing furball to have his way with.

I don't call Carlos. Papi's soccer buddy is a good guy, but he wouldn't be able to shield me from the sweaty bros I'd have to deal with all day long, working at a gym.

Instead I find myself searching online for Marguerite whatever-it-was, who Jess mentioned on the bus. Someone Summer was emulating when she expressed her desire to eviscerate some dudes. I have to try a few times to land on the spelling—the last name on Jess's tongue was something like Bress-you. Finally I find it: Marguerite de Bressieux.

I feel less ignorant for never having heard of her, because the internet doesn't know much more than I do. But what it knows is intriguing. It makes me itch for the Moleskine that's been sitting on my desk since I dug it out of my closet.

I'm passed out on the couch with Chester when Mom gets home.

"Hey, sweetie." She sinks into the tattered armchair, its scratched-up sides a memorial to Elinor's dearly departed feline. "Where's Papi? Did you get dinner? You fed Chester?"

"Plumbing emergency. Yes, and yes." I sit up slowly. "I'm going to bed."

She frowns. "It's only nine. You okay?"

None of us are okay.

Then her face brightens, her eyes light on the notebook in my lap. "I haven't seen that in forever! Are you journaling again?"

"It's nothing."

She always called it a journal, like I was writing to my dear diary about crushes and heartbreak and hopes and dreams. Maybe I was, in my way. But the specific word choice always irked me. I grab the not-journal and head for the stairs, Chester padding along behind me. "There's jocón and salad in the fridge, if you're hungry."

CHAPTER SEVEN

Because I have not suffered enough, Jess is on my bus the next morning.

"You are totally on the paper," they say, sliding into the seat next to me and holding their phone up to my face. "In fact, you're the editor next year. What are you doing here?"

Ms. Lim needs to update the website. "Going to school, like you I assume."

"School's out." They grin, flipping glossy black hair out of their eyes. "Ever the devoted, helpful student, I might also be hoping to score brownie points with Ms. Federighi by helping clean out the theater for the summer, and thereby increase my chances of being cast as Puck in the fall. How about you?"

I sigh and tuck my notebook into my bag. "Basically same. The paper staff is cleaning up the newsroom." Only difference is I'm way past scoring brownie points.

"See! You are on the paper!"

"Not next year. Don't believe everything you read."

"Oh." By some miracle, they're quiet for a minute. "I never read the *Oracle* before you started writing those profiles."

"Really?"

"It's just, like, sports, ugh. We'd read when the plays got reviewed. But that was it. One day, though, Summer couldn't put it down and I could tell it really mattered to her . . . Anyway, you did a good thing. Writing those. Your sister—"

"Thanks." It's nice of them to say, but not nice enough that I want to talk about Nor. "What do you know about Marguerite de Bressieux?"

Jess blinks long, glittery lashes slowly. "Um . . ."

"On the bus yesterday? With Summer? You said—"

"I remember." They study me in silence while the bus stops. People get on, people get off. "I get it if you don't want to talk about Nor. Sorry."

Only her closest friends call her Nor. I've been acquainted with Jess for years, but they were never in Nor's inner circle.

"So about our lady knight," they say. "Eavesdrop much?"

My cheeks flame.

"Kidding! I like to think everyone's always hanging on my every word. Marguerite was pretty badass. I mean, there's not much actual history about her—"

"Yeah, I looked."

"Then you probably know as much as I do. Are you into medieval shit? I've been wanting to start a club forever, but Mr. Lopez says a club needs at least three members to be official. I've only got Summer."

"I'm . . . no." Their disappointment is so palpable I muster some sort of interest. "What would you even do in a medieval club?"

They brighten. "Well, the obvious is Dungeons and Dragons. I'm not so into that. I'm more into real history. Which, it would be awesome if dragons were historical, but not a lot of paleontology to support that. But we could research things—like de Bressieux!—and make foods and costumes. I'm trying to get a cosplay together for the medieval faire in the summer, out on the peninsula."

I am less interested in making costumes with a medieval history club than assisting my dad on his next toilet explosion. I shouldn't have even brought Marguerite up; I only wanted them to stop asking about my sister. Elinor. Which is how they should have referred to her because nobody else is taking anything of Nor's unless she has expressly handed it to them.

That's when Summer gets on the bus, exasperated when she sees there's no seat next to Jess.

"Oh yay!" Jess says. "I won't be the only suck-up in the theater!"

"Go sit with her," I say.

Their face falls a little, but then they jump up and dive into the row Summer occupied. "Summer, my love!"

Someone across the aisle snickers and mutters something rude. I don't even have to hear the words to know the gist. They might think they're judging how Jess looks, or how Jess is different, but what they're really judging is the fact that Jess cares. About everything. With their whole heart.

Like I used to.

———

At school, Jess and Summer split off for the theater, where at least treachery and plot twists are expected. Inside the main building, Fremont High feels like a foreign land. School's been out less than a day and suddenly it's a ghost town.

As I draw closer to the newsroom, though, Sam's familiar cackle floats toward me. Nothing's changed for my friends. They texted their support, tweeted their outrage at the sentencing, cussed out the judge for a few days. It's not that they weren't genuinely upset. They were. But now they're off to Denver to geek out with other student journalists all summer. They'll come back and keep putting out the *Oracle*, like it matters. They'll go off to college. Some might even become journalists. Whatever that means.

I pause in the doorway, taking it in. I've spent more hours in this room than I can possibly remember. Even before I was in high school, Nor was on the paper. I used to walk over from the middle school and hang out on the slouchy couches in the corner while I waited for Nor to be finished and ready to walk home together.

Come freshman year, I already felt like I belonged and I made myself a permanent fixture until Ms. Lim put me on staff.

We didn't only put out a school paper in this room, either. We spent lunches here, gossiped, stressed, debated politics, railed against our parents, all of it. Ms. Lim always struck the right balance of being a presence we could rely on but also giving us a space where we didn't have to think about adults.

"Em!" Sadiqa looks over from where she's wiping down the white boards. "Hey, we missed you at Roxy's yesterday."

"Get over here, you!" Francie's personality has always been huge, but now it grates on me. When I don't bound over to where she and Sam are pulling things off the bulletin board, she comes to me, throwing her arms around me like we didn't have Spanish together less than twenty-four hours ago. "I was worried you weren't coming!"

"You would have survived." The room actually looks pretty good. Marco gives me a silent wave from the counter where he's washing out the coffee maker. "Where's Ms. Lim?"

"Ran to the office." Sam hands me a file box, but I don't know what I'm supposed to do with it.

I set the box down and drift past the wall covered in framed photos of each year's newspaper staff, stopping at the one where I'm a freshman and Nor's a senior. The first freshman on staff, and her sister, the lead photographer.

"Marianne, hey." Ms. Lim bumps my shoulder as she scoots past me toward her office, arms full, as always. She flips on the lights, dumps her stuff on her desk, and motions me in. "How are you, hon?"

Enraged. Helpless. Consumed by guilt. "Fine."

"Yeah? I'm glad you came by today. I thought we might not see you."

"It's required to finish the class."

She stops what she's doing and sits, motioning for me to sit too. I don't. "You're upset about Summer Intensive."

"No."

"Look, I get it. You worked hard for it all year. Harder than anyone would have asked you to, and you earned it. Right up until you posted that unauthorized article on the paper's website."

I don't want to rehash this again. I don't even want to go to Denver.

I'm also not sorry about the op-ed I posted on the *Oracle* site. Ms. Lim wouldn't let me write about my own sister's case because of conflict of interest and journalistic ethics or whatever. I get it, in theory. But nobody lacks conflict of interest when it comes to sexual violence. You're either biased by a constant awareness it could happen to you at any moment or you're biased by your privilege. Not to mention everyone knows someone who's been sexually assaulted.

So does that mean no one should write about it ever? That seems like a good way to maintain the status quo.

"You've had a nightmare year. And you've done amazing work throughout. That piece on sexual violence against trans people? I'm so proud of you. I hope we can move forward and have a great final year together, even if you're not editor. Quite frankly, that decision wasn't mine. The administration . . . But you'll still have loads of freedom to pursue the stories you want—"

"I'm quitting the paper."

Her movement stutters for a moment, and then she begins sorting through the pens in the mug on her desk, checking them for ink. "No, you're not," she says, calm as anything.

I clear my throat, try to remember the speech I planned. "I've given this a lot of thought. Journalism isn't what I want anymore. I need to take this year to . . . explore other things. Regroup. Figure out what I want to do in college. If I even want to go to college."

Ms. Lim's eyes flash as she struggles to maintain her composure. "You're not a quitter. I've been so impressed with you from the moment I met you, this indignant middle schooler invading my newsroom. But especially this last year, your fight has been extraordinary—"

"And it's amounted to nothing! There was no point to any of it!"

"I understand how you feel."

"I fucking doubt it, Ms. Lim."

"Marianne?" There's a harsh edge to her voice, more ragged than I've ever heard in three years of working on her paper. "Hear me when I say I understand how you feel."

Fact: One in three women in the United States experience sexual violence.

"Then you can understand why I'm done with the paper."

"I can't, actually. If you need to take a leave of absence—"

"I'm done."

It's not like it doesn't hurt, like I'm not flayed open here. But I've been flaying myself open all year long and it hasn't accomplished anything. At a certain point, quitting is mercy.

"Thanks for everything, Ms. Lim."

I hurry through the newsroom, avoiding the curious eyes. They'll have heard the raised voices. Sam and Francie will text before I'm out of the building. I'm barely out of the classroom when Ms. Lim calls out from the doorway, "Marianne? You do know how to use a sword."

CHAPTER EIGHT

My music's on so loud I almost don't hear the phone. I'm chopping chives for the risotto, checking on the pot roast, making the salad dressing. I'm not the family cook, but apparently Nor isn't, either. Not anymore. And we have to eat.

I only see the call because I splash olive oil on my phone and Nor's face appears right as I'm cleaning it off. Both of our faces, actually, on a boat crossing Lake Atitlán two years ago. I was terrified, the water choppy and the boat less than structurally sound. Nor was distracting me, telling stupid jokes and using her superior Spanish to flirt with some patojos behind us.

"Hello?"

As I fumble to turn down the music, I slip on a wet patch that means the kitchen sink is leaking again.

"Em?"

"Hey, sorry, I'm making dinner and I . . . How are you?"

"Um, okay? Just got back from a swim."

Even the most mundane things are loaded. Nor's a runner. Ran a marathon with Papi her senior year. Now she can barely do normal day-to-day activities without screaming pain all over her body. A physical manifestation of her trauma or some shit her naturopath told her. She suggested gentle swimming.

"What are you making?"

"What?"

"For dinner."

"Oh. Risotto. And pot roast."

"Ambitious."

I consider inviting her to come over to eat, but she'll only say no.

There's a pause. Then she says, "Have you talked to Mom?"

"No. About what?"

"Never mind." Another pause.

Talking to Nor never used to be awkward. When she went off to school, she was only across town, but we didn't live together anymore, so suddenly we were texting all the time and talking every afternoon or evening when we were both done with classes. Meeting in the U District for phở when I got a free afternoon away from the paper.

That lasted one semester. Until she went to a party at the SAE house after the Apple Cup.

"Papi said you're taking the job with Carlos at the gym?"

"I mean, maybe." I remember the risotto with a start and go to stir it. "Hey, were you ever friendly with Jess Stevens?"

"Who?"

"They're in my year. It's not important."

"Wait, I remember Jess. Purple hair, right? At least, last I saw them. I wouldn't say . . . friendly. But they helped me change a tire one day when I'd stayed late for layout and they were there for some theater thing. Why?"

"Oh, just. I saw them. They said hey." I want to ask her about school—about her oceanography program, her summer classes, her life. But everything leads back to Craig.

"Look, I know it sucks that you're not going to Denver. You kinda put Ms. Lim in a tough spot. But you'll still have the paper—"

"I quit the paper." She was going to find out sooner or later.

"Wait . . . what?"

"There's nothing to say, really. Just . . . I stepped down earlier today."

"What are you talking about? You've devoted yourself to the *Oracle* for three years! This doesn't make any sense."

"What doesn't make any sense is throwing all my energy into something pointless, that changes no minds and has no effect on the big picture."

She's quiet for a minute. I think maybe she's crying. "Is this about me?"

Of course it is, Elinor, because every fucking thing has revolved around you for the last year.

But I don't say that. I can't say that. She wouldn't have gone through all the scrutiny if I hadn't told her she should: She had to let them collect a rape kit; she had to agree to testify, convincing her there would be justice; she had to put herself in the spotlight for the good of womankind because if Craig had left her for dead behind the frat house, how many other girls would become his victims?

"It was my choice. It's what I want."

It's a low blow. She won't argue against my right to choose what I want. But suddenly I'm exhausted. And I've forgotten to stir the risotto again.

"Shit, Nor, I'm sorry, I'm at a stage with dinner where I need both hands . . ."

She sniffles. "Okay. I'm sure if you change your mind, Ms. Lim—"

"I won't."

As soon as we hang up, I'm choking on sobs I haven't let loose since before the trial. Chester's there, constant witness to suffering, or else hoping I'll drop a scrap of food. Either way, I sink to the kitchen floor and bury my face in his jet-black fur.

Chester, short for Mr. Rochester, named by Elinor in her *Jane Eyre* phase, back when she thought dangerous, brooding men were intriguing and mysterious. But Mr. Rochester's a perv and a cheater who keeps his mentally ill wife locked in the attic.

Chester the loveable furball nudges my face with his wet nose. I sob a little harder, hard enough that I don't hear the garage door open or my mom come into the kitchen. She appears around the edge of the counter and, not expecting to find me and Chester huddled on the kitchen floor, lets out a startled yelp.

I yelp back, then sob harder, until Mom is on the floor too, Chester between us.

"Oh, honey," she says, when our sobs die down. "I understand how you feel. After all she did to get into that program. It's so unfair."

I don't know what Mom's talking about, but it doesn't really matter because she's stroking my hair and she's here with me.

"She was nervous to tell you," Mom says. "So I'm glad she did. But I'm sorry you're taking it so hard. Is something burning?"

I leap up. The risotto is obviously ruined if culinarily clueless Mom can smell the charred bits melding onto the bottom of the pan.

"I wish she would move home, take some time off. She says that would be letting him win. But if he's run her out of the program she loves, isn't he already winning?"

"Out of the oceanography program?"

"She didn't tell you?" Mom's stricken. Somehow she's gone from being the sort of mother who throws her daughters menarche parties and takes their friends to Planned Parenthood to suddenly not knowing how to tell me the basic facts of my sister's life. "It just got a bit . . . untenable. He had a lot of friends in the program. And Nor's advisor made some comments . . ."

I haul the risotto pot over to the sink to dump its contents down the disposal.

"Oh, honey, no! I'm sure it's fine! We'll eat around the burned bits."

Nor dropped out of her oceanography program at University of Washington. Which she had been talking about since a seventh-grade field trip to the aquarium. The whole reason she chose the school where she met Craig. He's not even there anymore, but he'll always be there for her.

"There's salad in the fridge," I say, filling up the risotto pot to soak. "Pot roast in the slow cooker. I'm not feeling well."

———

The blues swirl into each other, faded shadows of the day Nor and I painted them years ago. She was about to start high school; oceanography was already her world. The mural is faded, and never was a work of art, if I'm honest. But it's still the undersea haven Nor wanted, her walls and ceiling swirling blues, with tendrils of seaweed creeping up around the edges of her bed, her desk, her dresser.

She took magazine photos of her favorite sea creatures and Mod-Podged them onto her walls. The clear Christmas ornaments suspended from the ceiling had been my idea, bubbles drifting toward the surface.

Whenever my friends slept over, they always wanted to sleep in Nor's room. She always let us.

When Nor left for UW, though, I stayed out. I wanted it to be perfect whenever she came back. Like we could slip back into our normal roles at any moment. Then Craig happened. Nor didn't come home. Lately I've been spending more time underwater than not.

Now Nor's done with the ocean. With this vast, unknowable thing she'd made it her life's mission to know. She won't see these creatures up close. She won't blaze new trails in the 95 percent of the ocean that's still unexplored.

Those discoveries are for men like Craig, men who supported him, who have one another's backs and then shrug when asked why there aren't more women in their field.

I pull my notebook from under Nor's pillow. I've opened it a few times since I dug it out of my closet. But my thoughts have been messy, incoherent things, impossible to boil down to something as mundane as words.

They aren't just thoughts, they're a swirling tornado of fury and hurt and fear and girl.

BLOODIED TAPESTRIES

ENGEANCE IS
my second thought.

First: my sister.

Did the monsters
crush her wings
to dust between
barbaric fingers,
a nuisance moth?

Or did the moth
flit away, fold
into a crevice
unseen, out of reach
like when we
were girls at play?

I'd wander the halls
in search of the sister
I'd find eventually
tucked away in a nook
blanket, book
our game forgotten.

What I do not

can not

consider in the mayhem
of the only home
I've ever known
turned upside down
iron on stone
bloodied tapestries
wreckage rubble ash

is my own wings.
Not so delicate
but like Helene's
meant for flight
not bondage.

Or perhaps
I could consider
my wings but

I won't.

NOT THREE STEPS
from my chambers,
my refuge until this day

I stumble on
wreckage
of another sort.

Not toppled statue
or broken window but

        Etienne

captain of my father's guard
a shout away from my door
sword useless at his side

he could be sleeping
if not for his guts spilling out
blood soaking the rug
that cushioned his fall.

This did not happen

only

        to

            me.

HELENE IS NOT
tucked in a corner
with a book.

Not in her chambers
oblivious to her role
as damsel, gazing out a window
on a world that would see her wings
pinioned on display and call them

beautiful.

MOTHER'S CHAMBERS
are still, a chapel
devoid of the faithful.

I turn to leave but stop
at the faintest scent
of the oils she rubs
behind her ears
fresh from a bath.

It lingers after
she leaves a room.
A memory, promise
of her return. It doesn't
mean she's here.

But in this chapel
a whispered prayer
pulls me back
makes me stay
tread lightly
through the rubble
around the bed—

                           dead

sprawled   in blood

                                 skirts askew

        empty gaze

here   but   not

If I should scream
will Father come running?
My brother? Sweet Helene?

I send heavenward
a plea to a god
I'm not sure is there,
crouch down and swipe
my mother's eyelids shut.

Then pull the brooch
from her shredded bodice
and run.

CHAPTER NINE

Words fly like I never buried this notebook in my closet, never stopped screaming my rage at boys who take what they want and burn down the rest. Screaming my rage into a notebook in a coffee shop, no one's going to try to silence me.

"Okay, here's what we're going to do."

At first I don't think anyone is talking to me. I'm sitting at Chocolati with Marguerite and the chai I've been nursing for an hour. I'm on one of the tall barstools at the counter reserved for loners who didn't come here to gab with a writing group or interview a prospective doula or hash out their relationships for all the world to hear.

But suddenly someone is sitting on the stool next to me, facing me. Talking as though I look like someone who wants to socialize, as though I don't have headphones on.

"My uncle is the crew coach. Well, assistant. But still he's in the department, so I'm thinking he could ask the athletic director to make a statement. I don't know, 'Kyle Cameron's decision to leave had been in the works for some time' . . . Something that takes the heat off Nor."

My head pops up. Jess Stevens drums black fingernails on the tabletop, waiting for me to catch up. "Are you following me?"

"What? No." They pop up when the barista calls their name. I scowl at their back as they retrieve their drink and doctor it at the counter.

I don't even want to know what they were talking about. I am so beyond caring what the Husky football coach does with his life.

"I came here to work," I say when Jess returns. "Alone. No offense. I just . . . have a lot going on."

"No shit. It's so fucking awful. I thought you might need help brain-storming what to do next."

I sigh, then start packing up my stuff. "Next? The judge made his rul-ing. There is no next."

Jess waves their hand like I'm talking nonsense. "Yeah, yeah, that ass-hole. No, I mean Cameron moving to Michigan State, the hashtag?"

I passed Head Coach Kyle Cameron in the courthouse on one of the last days of the trial—I was coming out of the women's bathroom as he went into the men's next door. His massive shoulder knocked me into the wall.

"Whoa, little lady," he boomed as he reached out to steady me by the elbow. "Watch yourself now."

He looked me straight in the face with zero recognition, even though I'd been sitting next to Nor the entire trial. If he'd glanced her way at all, he would have known I was her sister.

I shrug. "Serves him right if U Dub fired him. I'm sure he'll only fail up."

"Um." Jess scoots their stool closer to mine. "He wasn't fired. He left for a better program. Because of 'the distraction.' The football zombies are pissed."

Distraction: anything the people in power want to ignore.

"But that's . . . that's great! Isn't it?" I fumble for my phone, pull up the hashtag #JusticeforNor.

I haven't checked it for a few days. After the judge's sentencing, every-one moved on to being outraged about something else.

"Wait, hang on—" Something in Jess's voice makes me pause and meet their eyes. "I mean, sure, in the schadenfreude sense, it's pleasant to watch the meatheads denied something they thought they were entitled to. It might even look like consequences of some form. But . . ."

"Jess, what?"

"Some assholes, like, they're to be expected, right? You know it as well as I do. Maybe you didn't before the whole trial and everything, but you must know now, because, like, I only followed the coverage some of the time, but you must have—"

I grab my things and leave the coffee shop.

"Wait!" Jess follows me out. "Wait, sorry. I ramble when I'm nervous. Here's the thing: It's bad for the football program to lose their head coach."

I scan through the top search results for "Kyle Cameron" + "college football."

MICHIGAN STATE SCORES UNIVERSITY OF WASHINGTON HEAD COACH

CAMERON DEPARTS UW AMID OFF-FIELD DISTRACTIONS

Under one of the headlines, I read "'I want to focus on what matters,' says Cameron. 'And that's football.'"

"I still don't see why this is bad for Nor." I scan through #JusticeforNor. Nothing.

"It's bullshit, but like . . . football is life for some people." Jess reaches out, takes my phone, and types something in the search bar. "Are you sure you want to see this?"

I grab the phone. #IgNorTheWhore. It isn't only a few loser MRAs, either. This hashtag is constantly updating with new results. It'll probably be trending soon, if it isn't already.

Cowardly Cameron's dooming an entire football season on the word of one lying bitch. Good riddance. #IgNorTheWhore #PurpleReign

Just because that cunt Elinor Morales will lie down and take it doesn't mean Huskies will. #IgNorTheWhore

News flash for Cameron: There are lying sluts at Michigan State too. #IgNorTheWhore #GoHuskies

Title Nine? More like TITLE WHINE! Take your feminazi friends and go back where you came from! #IgNorTheWhore

Maybe Elinor Morales is working for Wazzu—cry rape, destroy
Lawrence, and maybe finally the Cougs can win some games.
#IgNorTheWhore #PurpleReign

My vision goes blurry. It's not tears. I'm way too enraged for tears. Jess's hand steadies my arm.

"Hey, are you—"

Then I'm crumpled on the sidewalk, breathing fast, trying to suck in enough air, but something isn't working right in my lungs or my brain or my—

"Marianne, should I call—"

This is my fault. The blaming, the look-what-she-wore, it was such bullshit when it was weaponized against her, but this time it really is my fault. If I hadn't pushed my sister—

Jess dials their phone. My hand shoots out and knocks it away from their hands.

"Sorry!" I blurt, reaching blindly for the phone.

"I got it."

"Don't call anyone. I'm fine."

"Okay." They start to rub my back, tentative at first. "Is this okay?"

I nod. "Don't go."

"I'm not going anywhere."

We sit there. After a minute, a shadow falls over us as a stroller stops. I don't look up.

"We're having a moment," Jess tells the person pushing the stroller. Or maybe the baby. When they've moved on, Jess says, "My therapist has me do this thing where I focus on two things I really like. She says two things that bring me joy, but whatever, two things I like. It can be anything. So it can be, like . . . hedgehogs and boba. Then I breathe in and out slowly, and when I breathe in, I think hedgehogs, and when I breathe out, I think boba. Just sort of say the words in my head. I don't, like, ponder the existence of boba."

Jess's words washed over me. Something about boba. But their voice is soothing. I focus on their voice and the steadiness of their hand on my back. There's somebody willing to sit on the sidewalk in Wallingford and not say awful things about my sister, and that helps a little.

"Can you think of two things you like? To do or eat or whatever?"

I process the words. I do. I even manage to reach through the flood of horrible words about my sister and try to wrap my fingers around something—anything—I like in this shitty, shitty world.

"Yeah," Jess says after a while. "I get it. Sometimes there's nothing to like."

———

Papi has seen the new hashtag. The aroma of rising bread tells me before I even walk in the door. My father had so many emotions to process during the trial that he mastered every variety of pan dulce, and then moved on to macarons, croissants, and croquembouche.

He tries to plaster on a smile when I walk in. "Hola, canchita. ¿Cómo estás?"

"Well, I've been on the internet, if that answers your question."

His face falls. "Your mother hasn't seen it."

He doesn't say let's call her. Or don't tell her. Probably because he doesn't know what to do, either. There's no point upsetting her, but would it be worse if she finds out later that we kept it from her?

Besides which, Mom teaches college. Probably some of her students are following the hashtags. She might find out in the middle of a lecture on colonial slut-shaming.

I reach for my phone. I keep meaning to change the lock screen. That photo of me and Nor at Lake Atitlán looks like something from another life, the wind whipping our hair into a swirl of dark strands and light, our identical smiles the only clue of our shared blood.

Of course, Nor must have seen those vile posts. She did a pretty good job of staying away from social media before, but someone would have told her. One of her friends, whoever she's talking to these days. Not me.

Maybe it doesn't matter. After everything, what are hashtags?

But Nor still lives on campus. People who are enraged about potentially lost football games are obviously not the most rational people.

"She needs to come home." I sink onto a stool. I hadn't intended to talk to Papi about it. But things keep happening that I hadn't intended.

"Mom?"

"No, Nor! What if they . . . do something?"

Papi sighs and drops his head into his hands, no bread challenging enough to process this. His elbows rest on the floury countertop. "¿Qué más hay?"

But there is more. There's always more. The horrors never end.

BLURRING FACES

FATHER IS A BOOK
splayed open
spine broken
no gold leaf
or knowledge, learning
sufficient to stanch
the flow of blood
from sword to gut.

Margot.

Always dominant
in stature, presence, voice
Father is small and frail
a few breaths from his last.

Philippe is hunting.
He will return, bring help.

A single bandage
cannot help a man
torn limb from limb.

Your mother?

No time to obfuscate;
Father reads my face
like pages in the books
around us and just as useless.
He sobs, grief forcing
the sword still deeper.

I grab his hand as though
I can hold him here
for one last lesson.
The cool weight of his ring
          our family crest
          our legacy
powerless to protect us,
presses into my hand.

          Helene?

This time I manage
an upturn of my mouth.

She's alive, Papa.
She's alive.

I SPEAK THE TRUTH:
> my sister will live
> until I kiss her eyes shut
> like Mother's
> and Father's
> and all I hold dear.

I could stop
hunker down
somewhere with
no corpses
and live awhile
in a world
where Helene is alive
where Father's ring
hangs heavy on my hand
because he has indulged me
one more time
that I could be
the hussy of this family
and not because I took it
off his lifeless finger.

NO SOONER
has possibility sunk
tendrils into the soil
of my grief than
it is yanked out
by the roots
replaced by a blight
of terror, creak of a door
within striking distance.

Striking distance
and me without
a weapon.

MADEMOISELLE?

Not blade but balm: Colette.
Colette who soothes, cajoles
and sands my roughest edges.
Bites her tongue
when required
but never holds back
when we are two
and doors are closed.

How could I have
forgotten Colette?

I fling open the closet
where linens are stored
and find her curled
among sheets and blankets
a gash across her cheek
dripping onto rich brocade.

Colette...

The servant girl
bursts into tears
at the sight of me
her mistress.

*I thought there was
no one left.*

Me too.

I kneel, gather
her in my arms.

Oh, me too.

CHAPTER TEN

What comes next is too awful to face, so I wander away from the words in search of food. Papi sits alone at the kitchen counter, eating a bowl of cereal. Cereal. Not even fancy granola he made himself with artisanal honey and sprouted oats. Just some crap that came out of a box with anthropomorphized grains on the front.

"You okay, Papi?" I rummage in the fridge. Supplies are low. "Hey, are you going to the store soon?"

"¿Por qué no vas vos? Now that your summer is wide-open, maybe you could pitch in a bit more."

My summer isn't wide-open. Not now that I have to tell Marguerite's story. "I can if you want. I thought you liked to have control over the grocery shopping. Remember the white-onion-yellow-onion debacle?" I pull out the carton of eggs, empty save for a light gray speckled egg produced by one of the chickens next door.

"Lo siento." He rubs his face and then leaves his head resting in his hands, like Atlas holding up the entire world.

I crack the egg into a pan on the stove and clear Papi's dish away. "You need coffee?"

"Siempre."

I don't make magic in the kitchen like Nor, but I do like the predictability. The routine. Grind the beans, boil the water, pour it over the grounds, voilà: coffee. Sure, the result could vary depending on the type or freshness of the beans, the amount of water, some other variables, probably. But I'm never going to go through those steps and end up with yogurt or kombucha. It will always be coffee, come what may.

"Want to make me a list and I'll bike to PCC?"

Papi lifts his head from his hands. "No, gracias. I'll go on my way back from my afternoon appointment."

I look around the cluttered living area. Most of it is Mom's clutter and she gets mad if anyone else tries to organize it. "I'll vacuum," I offer.

"Gracias, mija."

⸻

After I've vacuumed, I settle back on my bed with Marguerite. But the words won't come. I can envision the attack, but what comes after is somehow worse. Everyone seems to think those moments behind the frat house were the most awful of Nor's life. But Nor doesn't even remember that. The worst, she said, was when she woke up in the filthy alley, stripped down, broken ribs, and a used condom next to her the only indication of what had happened. That's when the nightmare began.

I mop the kitchen and bathroom next, as though by cleaning every surface in the house, I might uncover my way forward in the story. Can I do it justice, what Marguerite and Colette have been through?

Putting that horror into words almost diminishes it. How do you articulate a primal scream? I consider skipping ahead to a later point, but that feels like cheating. It isn't right, it isn't fair to skip over what Nor didn't have the luxury of skipping. What Marguerite had to endure.

I'm sweeping the front porch when Jess walks up with a cat on a leash.

"Cinderemma!" they say.

This time they're obviously talking to me, but it takes me a minute to process what they've said. "Em's not short for Emma. It's Marianne," I say. "Do you live around here?"

"My aunt Clare does. This is her cat, Vlad. We're having our daily constitutional."

"You take your aunt's cat on a daily walk? On a leash?"

They grin and squat down to scratch the cat behind the ears. "A couple times a week. But it's not as catchy to say our biweekly constitutional."

Biweekly: both twice a week and every other week. Because
sometimes the most precise word choice is still completely wrong.

Inside the house, Chester starts barking his head off, no doubt having
caught sight of the cat. On a leash, no less—the rare cat Chester might
have a chance of catching.

When I was little we had a cat named Bingley, and Chester was
deeply in love with it. They slept curled up together, shared treats; it was
weird. And ever since Bingley moved on to the great cat tower in the
sky, Chester has been in search of someone to fill the cat-shaped hole
in his heart.

"You have a dog?" Jess says. "Vlad loves dogs." At the look on my face,
they grin even wider. I get the feeling Jess lives for a reaction, no matter
what that reaction is. "Vlad's a very unique cat."

I fight a smile. "Like you."

"Meow."

"I would invite Vlad inside, but Chester's a little unpredictable."

"Gotcha." Jess unhooks the cat from the black leather harness. "See
you at home, Vlad." The cat bolts down the sidewalk and disappears
around the corner.

"He doesn't need to be on a leash?"

"Who does? Unless you're into that sort of thing. No judgment."

"I mean, if he's an outside cat, why does he need to be walked?"

Jess shrugs and sits down on the porch steps. "Just because he can walk
alone doesn't mean he should have to. Plus, I kind of like the stares I get
when I'm walking a cat."

I'm basically done sweeping the porch, but I keep going over the same
spot. What are they even doing here? Francie and Sam never drop by
without notice. Is Jess my friend?

"I wanted to check on you," they say when I finally sit down. "After
Chocolati. The sidewalk?"

"I'm sorry—"

"I'm the one who should apologize! I thought maybe there was something we could do, but I only upset you."

I stare across the street at Mrs. Zackey's perfect rosebushes. "Why do you care so much?" About everything. "About Nor?"

"Well, for one thing, I can be insufferably nosy. But I think the better question is . . . why don't most people care more?"

And that's it—I have to write what comes next because most people wouldn't care enough to write it. Because it would be easier to ignore what comes next and fuck easy.

Suddenly I'm dying of thirst. "Do you want to come inside?"

In the kitchen, I busy myself with pulling out our cold drink options: sparkling water; lemonade; this weird carrot-orange juice blend my mom likes in the morning.

Jess sits at the counter, arranging the figures of a little clay Nativity set that sits out year-round, not because anyone in my family is especially religious, but because Mom got it on her first trip to Guatemala to meet Papi's family. "Nor was nice to me," Jess says. "During a time when a lot of people were pretty shitty. It stuck with me. I'd like to think I'd care about what happened to her even if she hadn't been nice to me first. But if you need a reason, I guess that's it."

Now they're adding Mom's trio of little gray ducks made from Mount St. Helens ash to the worshippers at the manger. They catch my eye, dare me to challenge the right of water fowl to attend the Christ Child's birth.

I pour sparkling water for Jess and get a glass of regular water for myself. "I want to know more about medieval stuff," I say.

It takes me all of five minutes to confess that I'm writing about Marguerite, and Jess doesn't bat an eyelash. They take it seriously, like of course I've decided to write a novel about this obscure historical figure. It's more energizing than I would have imagined, having someone believe it's not a completely ridiculous endeavor.

By the time Mom and Papi pull up, Jess is showing me this website about people of color in medieval art.

"Books and movies make it look like medieval Europe was all totally white, but that's bullshit. There were loads of Africans at all class levels. So if you're writing an authentic story, your medieval cast of characters shouldn't be all white."

I ponder what I've got so far. "I could make Colette African."

"Who's Colette?

"Marguerite's maid. I mean, she's fictional. We don't know anything about the people in Marguerite's life."

"Yeah, of course." Jess is quiet for a minute. "But do you want the first African character in your story to be a servant?"

"Oh." The thing is, Marguerite is a noble in a house full of servants. Her entire family is dead. There is no one else.

"It's something to consider," Jess says. "The roles we're given."

The front door opens on Papi making soothing sounds while Mom rants about something. "I honestly don't know if these kids don't believe I'll check if their papers are plagiarized or if they just don't care!"

They both walk in, arms full of groceries. "Hello there," Papi says.

Jess leaps up like royalty has entered the room. "Hello, Marianne's parents. I'm Jess."

"Jess," Mom repeats. "I'm sorry. I don't usually rant about my students in front of company." A horrified look crosses her face. "You're not a student at Central, are you?"

"They're in my year," I offer. "At Fremont."

I tell them Jess uses they/them pronouns and Papi nods. "Are you on the paper, Jess?" he asks.

"No, sir. I'm more of a theater nerd."

Papi raises his eyebrows. "Sir? I like that. But you can call me Andrés." He starts unloading the groceries.

"I'm Kath." Mom sinks into the chair next to Jess. "And freshman English compositions are going to be the death of me."

"Mom teaches lit at Central."

"Marianne!" Jess exclaims, pointing at me. "And Elinor! I just got it!"

Mom laughs with delight. "Did you? Few people do."

"*Sense and Sensibility*, right? Perfect for the English professor's daughters."

"Andrés chose the names," Mom says. "I prefer Brontë. But Jane and Shirley aren't such pretty names."

"I'm with you, sir," Jess says. "Andrés, I mean. Austen is queen. Marianne's the Kate Winslet one, right?"

"Yes," Papi says, abandoning the groceries. "The movie is excellent but you must read the book!"

"Papi—"

"Oh, I have!"

And then the medieval websites are abandoned as Jess and Papi bond over their shared love of Austen's social commentary, her deliciously bitter wit, her examination of power structures.

I want to love Austen. Brontë too. Trailblazing female authors and all. Except I can't help but think their romantic leads were all—these men who are supposed to be so desirable—abusive jerks and creepers.

———

"Who's the goodest boy? Chester's the goodest boy."

Jess sprawls across my bed, snuggling Chester. They've bonded in record time. Possibly because of the amount of cat hair always clinging to Jess's clothes. It definitely isn't the vegan dog treats they bring every time they show up. Which has been almost every day in the last week.

"Do you ever walk this dog? You should walk this dog. Want to go for a walk right now?"

I close the notebook and bang my head on top of it.

"Sorry. I'll be quiet."

They totally won't.

"Or we could take him to a dog park. We can't take him on the bus, though. Unless he's a therapy dog, which he totally could be. He's absolutely serving me Dogtor Freud vibes right now. Do you have your license? I don't have my license."

I try to keep the edge out of my voice when I say, "Why don't you walk him? His leash is on a hook in the kitchen."

"Are you trying to get rid of me, Marianne Dashwood?"

I bang my head less gently.

"Okay, fine. Chester and I know when we're not wanted. But when we get back, you are paying attention to me because breaks are an important part of the creative process."

"Also because Summer has abandoned you and you're needy."

"Ouch," they say, turning back in the doorway. "But accurate."

Right around the time Jess started showing up at my house, Summer left for an expensive theater program she and Jess have always done together, but this year Jess can't.

"Divorce is expensive" is Jess's only explanation.

With some peace and quiet, I write a little bit more. I've decided to try making Marguerite's servant Colette Ethiopian—a well-represented immigrant group in France at the time—so I'm rethinking her character and naming her Zahra. But then I get stuck on the layout of the castle. Jess would know. I grab my phone to search for the answers I need and try not to linger on my lack of notifications.

No word from Nor must mean she's okay. If she weren't, I'd know.

She'd tell me.

I think.

What happened to her didn't happen to me. It doesn't compare, not even a little bit. I'm an asshole for even thinking this, but: I lost something huge that day too.

SCAFFOLDING

ALL IS NOT LOST.

Zahra's survival means
my heart does not beat
alone within these walls;
perhaps my sister survives.

The urge to tear
the castle stone from stone

            as though it is not
            already in ruins

wars with my loyalty
to Zahra. Born into service
weeks after my noble birth,
our lives have been
entwined from the first.

Sure-footed Zahra is
unsteady on her feet.
Our world is upside down,
I take my servant's weight.

What is it?
What can I do?

A careful inventory
reveals ripped dress
bloody skirt
face that will scar

for the rest of her life
if she lives long enough
for tissue to form.

Where are you hurt?

Zahra can't meet my eye.
Zahra, who bathes me
scrubs my bloody rags.

>   *Between my legs,*
>   she finally says.

I TAKE HER HANDS.

They hurt me too.

       So many.

I know.

       I should have—

No.

No time for blame.

I will not leave you
but we must go.

Together we stumble
like Philippe on the bottle
but our foreign limbs
precarious steps
come not from what
we've chosen to consume.

My servant, my sister's
bones and muscles, sinew, skin
weigh little more than air
and yet the crushing weight
of soldiers laughing
trousers around ankles
armor shielding them
is still upon us both.

THE GRAND STAIRCASE
is a battlefield.
Zahra must rest
every few steps
but sitting exposed
is worse than
the throbbing pain
of constant motion.

No audience
for our descent
except another maid
huddled behind a table.
She joins us
without a word.
There are no words.

We search each nook
where Helene might hide,
find two more women
streaked with blood
and grime and horror.

Finally the kitchen
castle epicenter
source of sustenance.
The servants are at home
but I'm on foreign soil.

And still without Helene.

BETSY HOLDS COURT
wielding a massive knife,
hair a wild halo, avenging angel.

The head cook tenses
at our arrival then
slumps back down
at the sight of us
half rising when
she notes my presence.

Betsy, have you seen
Lady Helene?

No, mademoiselle.

Formality, titles feel absurd
when all else has been wrenched away.
But perhaps the structure of our stations
will be a scaffolding
on which we all can cling.

I think some tea
might do us well.

THE CLINK AND CLATTER
as Betsy moves about
a horrible echo
of sword on sword
and barricades breached.

Breathe, remember,
her aim is tea

              not carnage.

My parents who brought me
into this world
are dead.
Helene with them
in a place with no tea

or carnage.

Perhaps Philippe too
for I find no comfort
in the thought
of what lies beyond
these blood-soaked walls.

I may be the

only
one
left.

THE FIRE BLAZES
tea scalds my tongue
but the chill up my spine
pays no heed.

Gathered around the table:

Zahra, shattered, faithful,
the slightest color
warming her cheeks,
grip still tight on my arm.

Betsy of the perpetual scowl
who once brained a petty thief
with a cast-iron pan
for stealing fresh baked bread.

Three more women
gathered along the way.
Two whose names
I barely know.

The third, Matilde,
old as the stones
that witnessed the slaughter

witness to my mother's birth
now nearly blind
retained because Mother
is severe, but she is not
without a heart.

Was not.

WHAT AM I TO DO,
responsible for
all these women?

Motionless now
the ragged edges of the horror
reach out
                    snag upon my skin.
An easy target,
doe lapping at a stream
inviting the hunter's arrow

and yet

I cannot move.

CHAPTER ELEVEN

I am sprawled on the couch when Mom arrives with takeout, which is the first sign something's off.

"Where's Papi?"

"Hello to you too, my darling daughter." She dumps the bags on the kitchen counter and stomps back to their bedroom.

I get up to investigate the food. When Mom wants me to know what's wrong, I'll know. Plus the smell of Gordito's wafts from the bags. They have these burritos that are literally as big as a baby. The restaurant has photos on the wall of infants lying next to these monster burritos for comparison. We used to get a single burrito and split it four ways for the whole family.

Inside the bag I find three separately wrapped foil packages.

When the door slams, I wonder if Mom slipped out her bedroom window to come around and make another pissy entrance. But this time it's Papi. Who also has takeout bags.

He doesn't slam them on the counter like Mom, though. He stands frozen, staring at me in confusion. "Is that . . . for you?" He chin points at the three burritos I'm putting onto plates.

"For . . . all of us, I assume? Mom brought them home."

That unfreezes him. He drops his bags on the counter and stomps off to their bedroom. There's no way to avoid their rising voices in our tiny house. Plus, I'm kind of curious. I can count on one hand the number of times I've heard them yell at each other.

Papi's bags contain Korean. I start transferring the food to bowls.

"I said I'd get dinner!" Papi says.

"You said you wouldn't have time to make it!"

"And that I'd pick something up!"

"You were being sarcastic!"

"Why would I be sarcastic about that?"

I whistle at Chester to follow me so he doesn't sneak any food off the table, and we march to their bedroom. I knock on the door, but open it without waiting for a response. They both turn to me in shock.

"Jess is coming over in twenty minutes," I inform them. "Their parents have actual reasons to scream at each other in bedrooms, given the bitter divorce and all, so they get enough of whatever this is. There is an abundant multicultural feast getting cold on the table, so whatever this is? Maybe it can wait."

With that, I return to the table, where I start serving myself bibimbap. This could go any number of ways. We're all sort of spelunking without a headlamp here. After a shocked silence, they both explode in laughter and I breathe a sigh of relief.

They give explanations for their short tempers over dinner, even though the real explanation is we're all fried down to the last wire and could spark at any moment. They ask questions about Jess's home life, and I remind them of Jess's pronouns when they mess up. Papi ponders how to handle nonbinary pronouns in Spanish, which is so heavily gendered.

By the time Jess arrives, my parents are cleaning the kitchen together, talking about taking a salsa class at the community center.

———

"You're so lucky." Jess props their feet up on the railing along the back porch.

It's that time of year when the evenings stretch further and further and sometimes it seems like darkness will never fall.

But it always does eventually.

I know what they mean, so I don't say something snarky. I *am* lucky, in so many ways. I breathe in the last blooms on the neighbor's lilac tree while Jess's pencil scritches along a sketch pad.

"Can I see?"

"Not yet."

Chester perks up at the sound of a siren in the distance but decides it's not worth his while and settles back down at Jess's feet.

When we were little, anytime we heard a siren, Nor and I used to stop whatever we were doing, no matter what, and turn to each other, clasping both hands, and say, "Fire, sickness, horror, flood, sisters always, heart and blood."

I have no idea where it came from. Some creepy fairy tale, probably.

"Has your dad moved out yet?" I ask Jess.

Instead of answering, they hold up the sketch pad. They've drawn an amazingly intricate sword, the hilt engraved with curlicues and letters I can't read, the blade somehow catching the light, even though it's sketched in pencil.

"That's gorgeous."

"It's meant to be terrifying."

"Well, yeah. If it was pointed at my neck, it would be less gorgeous."

On the table between us, Jess's phone buzzes. They glance at a text, grimace. "Can I spend the night here?" When I don't answer right away, they add, "I don't have to if it's weird. It just sounds like they're still at it."

The relief I feel at the idea of late-night whispers, a person who'd wake if I wake, rushes in so fast it floods me with guilt. Jess is not a replacement for Nor.

"Of course you can."

I leave the notebook I've been holding like a shield on the table and go inside to pull out some extra blankets and arrange the hide-a-bed in the living room. I half expect Jess to follow me in and chatter up a storm while I make up a bed. But for once they stay still and quiet, alone except for Chester and the distant sirens.

Fire, sickness, horror, flood.

Once I'm done, I make hot cocoa and fill my parents in. They're all sad, concerned faces, but at least they don't go out to the patio to smother Jess with loving kindness.

When I get out there with two mugs of cocoa, Jess's pencil is back to scratching away.

"Another sword?" I ask, setting the cocoa down. Then I see that they're not drawing on their sketch pad. They're writing in my notebook. Cocoa sloshes across the table, spattering Jess's abandoned sketch pad as I grab Marguerite from their hands. "What the hell?!"

"What?!"

"You can't write in someone else's journal!"

"And you can't pour coffee all over someone's sketch pad!"

"That was an accident! And it's hot cocoa!"

The ridiculousness of that distinction dampens my fury, but only a little. "This is private."

"You've been asking for my help on every little thing! What kind of sword? What's the castle layout? Clothing? Armor? Where they'd take a shit!"

I take a careful breath, notice my parents watching us from inside. "That still doesn't make it okay for you to write in my book."

They nod. "Okay. You're right. I'm sorry. I should have asked. But I didn't write; I drew."

That doesn't make it better. But it does make me curious. I open the notebook and flip through until I find a page that contains not only my sprawling handwriting, but also a striking medieval sword over an intricate flowered tapestry, ripped and jagged at its bottom edge. But it's also this incredibly beautiful piece of miniature art.

I glance up. Jess watches carefully, more vulnerable than I've ever seen them.

"It's beautiful."

They let out a breath. "I was thinking about illuminated manuscripts? Do you know . . . ?"

I shake my head and sit while Jess pulls up some images on their phone. I'm looking at ornate pages from books—really old manuscripts from way before the printing press. The words look like calligraphy, but what's notable about these pages are the intricate borders, miniature illustrations, and gorgeous letters beginning each page.

"Illuminated, because they always had some gold leaf involved," Jess says, reaching over to scroll through and point out a favorite.

"They look religious."

"A lot are. Originally monks made them. Like, there were monks whose whole job was making these beautiful works of art. But by Marguerite's time, they weren't only religious. Books became status symbols. They were superexpensive, because of all the labor."

"And the gold leaf."

"Right. They sort of fell out of fashion when the printing press came along. But that was after Marguerite."

I scroll through some more of the photos. They're absolutely stunning. I'm not really a fine-art person, but I can't stop looking at these, all the detail, all the time poured into them. Books as status symbols, stories valued so much they were cast in gold.

"Marguerite's story is worth illuminating," Jess says carefully.

"Yeah. It is."

FLAY

THE CRACK OF A TWIG
alerts the doe
she's no longer
safe at the stream.
A man's shout
propels me to my feet.

Some dive for shelter
while Betsy wields her knife;
one of the new girls
grabs a broom, I grasp
for something, anything
but this is not an armory
and there's no time.

A man bursts through
the door; a surge of fury
sends me lunging, clawing
at his face, but Betsy
yanks me back.

Master Philippe!

MY BROTHER'S WILD EYES
and his desperation are
blunt-edged reminders
our parents have been slaughtered, and—

Helene?

He barely sees me, hell-bent on
the only survivor who matters.

I haven't . . .
I couldn't—

My brother's voice tears a sob
from my gut, the crescendo
of a keening wail that started
the moment the first dragon
breathed its all-consuming fire.

I never cried as a child
when he cut off my braids,
stole my sword, bested me in races.

My cry pierces his armor, brings
him to his knees as well.

I THOUGHT SHE'D STAY ALIVE
until I found her, blessed her
but wading through the massacre
has erased all doubt.

Helene is dead.

Philippe sees but doesn't
the women all around us
stripped to their cores
with nothing left but horror.

He asks not after Mother, Papa;
if either lived all eyes
would turn toward them.

Helene is dead.

I don't realize
how desperately
I long for embrace
until he reaches out
but only yanks me
to a corner.

> *You must take these women.*
> *Go immediately*
> *to the Sisters at Salette.*
> *One day's ride to the south.*
> *You'll be taken care of there.*

I cannot stay in this fortress of horrors
but neither can I set out on the open road.
Both prospects terrify in equal measure.
What life awaits me in a convent?
What death awaits me in the world?

AND WHAT OF YOU?

        Me?

There's the Philippe I know
looking at his kid sister
as though she were ridiculous.

        I'm going to find these bastards
        and flay them open, end to end.

Before I can argue, he's gone.
I'm left with the task of shepherding
these women, injured, traumatized,
into the mountains.

But

        you'll be safe there.

We aren't safe now.
Even if the monsters don't return
the life we knew here
has been drowned in blood.

CHAPTER TWELVE

"Maybe we could do the whole thing in the traditional style. Like, use the same sort of parchment and ink and stuff. When you're done writing."

Since I've started letting Jess doodle in the margins of my draft, they have been moping about their parents a lot less. Still sleeping over at my house more than half the time, though. The second night they fell asleep in my room, and we haven't bothered with the hide-a-bed again. Which has led to pointed questions from my parents, who fall all over themselves telling me how much they like Jess. "We want you to know you can always talk to us about stuff," Mom said yesterday, curiosity barely concealed.

Jess's focus on what Marguerite's story might be when it's finished is kind of antithetical to what I'm doing. I don't know what it'll be; I don't know if it'll ever be finished.

But I'm letting them drag me downtown to look at illuminated manuscripts.

A woman wearing everything she owns gets on the bus and slides into the seat in front of us. Jess digs around in their bag and when we're getting off at the next stop, they hand her a ten-dollar bill.

"I thought divorce was expensive," I say as we step onto the busy sidewalks of downtown.

They shrug. "Not as expensive as poverty in Seattle." Looping our arms together, they pull me toward the Seattle Art Museum.

The woman on the bus has somewhere to sit, unbothered, out of the sun for a while. I'm startled by how many tents line the streets, even in this swanky part of downtown. Somehow I didn't notice when we were here for the trial. Maybe these people, stripped to nothing in a city built on so much opulence, stay away from the courthouse because clearly justice is not in their favor.

Or maybe I didn't notice because I was too wrapped up in my own thing.

"Can I tell you a secret?"

I roll my eyes. Jess asks permission for a lot of things, but spilling their heart all over me is not usually one of them. "Always."

"I could have gone to camp. I mean, divorce *is* expensive. My parents are absolutely screwing themselves in screwing each other. But it would have been worth a few thousand to get me out of their hair for the summer."

"So why didn't you go?"

"I guess I thought I might keep them from killing each other. You always hear about people staying together for the kids, right? If I was right there, maybe they'd make more of an effort. Lord, what fools these mortals be."

They bump my shoulder toward the entrance of a massive, shiny glass building in the heart of downtown.

"It's not foolish to want to help the people you love." I reach for my wallet as we approach the ticket window at the museum.

"First Thursdays are free," Jess says, waving at the lady in the booth and pushing through the doors into a blast of air-conditioning.

Jess gives a friendly wave to the security guard, like maybe they come here all the time. Maybe they come with Summer, when she's not off at theater camp. Or maybe this is something Jess does alone, but now they're letting me in, like I've let them into my book.

No one's in the *Illuminated Manuscripts* exhibit. Probably not a huge demand to see medieval religious texts on a weekday morning, but people don't know what they're missing.

When I think of manuscripts, I think of words on pages, mostly. Like the Constitution or pictures of the King James Bible. They look cool because they're written in flowery script, but otherwise, they're only text.

These are different.

They're song books and prayer books and calendars, Bibles and histories and sometimes documents I can't decipher (mainly because they're in Latin or French). They're written in beautiful calligraphy, with very few words on a page, in most cases. Which makes sense, because the art needs room to shine.

In person, the manuscript pages are so much more stunning than the images online. The gold leaf on most of the pages shimmers magically, making them look not only valuable, but almost holy.

Sometimes the images depict familiar scenes—Madonna and Child, David slaying Goliath. Other times strange, indecipherable things are happening. A woman is harvesting . . . fruit? . . . from a tree that seems to produce penises.

And sometimes the illumination isn't a specific illustration— sometimes it's intricate designs surrounding the text. Flowers, vines, fleurs-de-lis, beautiful adornments I don't even know how to describe.

On some, the first letter of the text takes up the entire left-hand page, a giant, intricately decorated letter *B*, before the right-hand page continues the word: *–ehold*.

They're really, really breathtaking.

"Can you imagine how long these must have taken?" I say. Days for even a single page, I think. The love my parents have for words, for stories, the way they've built their lives around them, these take that passion to a whole other level.

"Forever. And multiple monks worked on each page. Sometimes they left little notes in the margin, complaining about their hand cramps. One says, 'Just as the sailor yearns for port, the writer longs for the last line.'"

I don't long for the last line, though. I might even dread it. But the monks who created these works of art weren't telling their own stories. Maybe that's the difference.

"Was it only monks?"

"Mostly, until books became a more commercial product. But there were female scribes too. Orders of nuns who worked like the monks. And the earliest-dated manuscript about Lancelot was written by a female scribe in the thirteenth century. We know because it ends with a line asking the reader to pray for the scribe. And uses a feminine pronoun to refer to her!"

Could that scribe have imagined two people would be discussing her work eight hundred years later? Would know at least something of her identity, or care?

It's not a very big exhibit and by the time I've rotated through all the manuscripts in the room, Jess is still standing at the very first page they stopped at.

It makes sense, I guess. They're the artist. I've always been about the words. I appreciate visual art, but sometimes I feel like I don't get it. And then, if I'm honest, that makes me feel sort of inferior, like I'm not sophisticated enough to get it.

Jess traces their finger on the glass, along the curving line of a gold-leaf vine. I return to the page they're still looking at. It's written in Latin, but I'm guessing from the angels it's a Bible. Or a prayer book. Jess is looking at it with a reverence I haven't seen from them before.

"Are you religious?"

I know they've heard me because their finger stops its path across the glass. But they're quiet for a bit.

"My nana used to take me to her church," they finally say. "I loved the choir, the organ. The giant stained-glass windows. And the way Nana would parade me around after, introducing me to all her friends and letting me eat as many of those pink and white circus animal cookies as I wanted.

"I get why lots of people don't feel this way, and maybe it was Nana or maybe it was her church, but I always felt safe there, you know? Welcome."

They finally move on to the next page. It isn't religious—this one is written in French, and I can make out enough words to know it's a calendar listing feast days. But they still stare at it like it's holy.

"Did she die? Your nana?"

"Last summer. She was in a home for her last few years and I was the only one who ever went to visit her." They pause. "People are so fucking awful. But they also make things so beautiful they break your heart, you know?"

————

We're at the Starbucks closest to my house, despite Jess's grumblings about corporate overlords. I get it. But sometimes I like how every Starbucks is exactly the same. When I walk in, I know what's on the menu. I know how to order. I don't have to decipher a million cutesy new names for the same old drinks, written on a smudged chalkboard.

I'm researching siege warfare while Jess draws an illuminated family crest. Or not technically illuminated, since they're not using gold leaf. Unless gold Sharpie counts? I think it's a Bressieux crest until I look closer and see a dog that looks remarkably like Chester, alongside a cat on a leash.

"Is that . . . Vlad?"

They grin and turn their sketchbook around so I can see more clearly. "Vlad and Chester, together on the page, as they never shall be together in this life."

The crest is divided into four sections, one of which is filled by Vlad and Chester. One includes theater masks and spotlights and curtains. One includes a sullen girl I'm pretty sure is Summer and an angry girl—

"Is that me?"

"Yes?"

"What am I doing on that crest?"

"It's my crest. My chosen-family crest."

My heart almost explodes.

"Shut up," they say. "I also included your big, dumb dog."

I hide my grin and search my medieval history book for something to change the subject. "So according to the code of chivalry, inhabitants of a castle were supposed to be allowed safe conduct out during a siege."

"Okay . . ." They keep drawing.

"So Marguerite and all the others should have been let out before the Prince of Orange and his men stormed the castle. Unless . . . what? Her father made them stay?"

"Possible. Overconfident in their defenses?" Jess sets down their pencil. "But I'm sure the code was broken all the time. It's not like Chalon was known as an honorable guy."

It's almost worse for a reasonable code to exist and be ignored.

"That's very unfair to all the dudes who seized what wasn't theirs in a peaceful and orderly fashion," I point out.

Jess snorts and goes back to drawing.

"I'm getting another chai. Do you want anything?"

They shake their head, unwilling to further line the pockets of the coffee barons.

I've just gotten in line when someone stands behind me, a little too close. But if I move forward at all, I'll be crowding the girl in front of me. It's obviously a guy, based on the toxic fumes of cheap cologne.

Toxic: the OED's 2018 Word of the Year, appearing most
frequently alongside 1) chemical and 2) masculinity.

I consider stepping out of line and getting my drink after this asshole has gone, but I don't want him to have any power over me.

The girl in front of me is ordering six different drinks and I swear this guy is slow-dancing close. I steal a look over my shoulder, to figure out if he's someone I want to give a withering look or full-on tell off. Then I realize why the cheap cologne was familiar.

"Marianne Morales! Man, it's been a while!"

Not long enough.

"I mean, I saw you on the news, but you weren't feeling so hot that day, were you?" He guffaws and slings a massive arm around my shoulder. "Looking hot now, though."

I extricate myself, give him the tiniest smile, which I immediately hate myself for—why should I give him anything—and head back to where Jess sits, watching.

"What?" Phil calls after me. "What'd I say?!"

"He looks like a charmer," Jess says as I sit and scowl at men in general.

"I dated him for about five minutes freshman year. He's harmless."

"Then why do you look so upset?"

He was a senior football player who took me to prom as a freshman. I was an idiot and thought I was special; I had no idea I was low-hanging fruit. He didn't rape me, and that's a pretty low bar for a decent human being.

"Let's forget him," I say, opening my book again.

Once he realized I wasn't going to put out and dropped me, Phil didn't say another word to me for the rest of his high school days. I keep my eyes on my book and don't look up until I smell another wave of that awful cologne.

"Hello, sir," Jess says in a jaunty tone. "What can we do for you this lovely day?"

Phil pulls up a chair and flips it around, straddling it like we invited him to sit in the most douchey way possible.

"Marianne Morales," he booms again, basically announcing my presence to the coffee shop. "Girl reporter. Are you hot on the trail of your next big scoop?"

"No, but I am busy right now." I shoot a look at Jess that means *do not provoke this asshole, it'll only be harder to get rid of him* and hope desperately that they understand.

Phil reaches out and pulls Marguerite across the table to look at what Jess is doing. I grab the notebook and flinch when my fingers brush his.

"We've still got a spark," he says with a grin. "Electric. But I'm not sure what my brothers would say if I brought you around the frat house."

Jess takes in a sharp breath. I freeze. *Around the frat house.*

"Hey, Em, we've got to get going if we're going to catch that bus."

"Aw, don't run off on my account. Was that rude? It's not that they wouldn't like you! But Big Sis kind of pissed off a lot of Husky fans. And Greeks."

Jess bolts to their feet and it's the first time I really register how tall they are. No match for Phil's football-playing hulk as he slowly stands, but still. Eyes blazing, Jess keeps their tone light as they say, "You can fuck all the way off, my friend."

Phil locks eyes with them. People are watching. Phil wears Husky football gear and while it doesn't matter what the dawgs or their minions do in dark alleys, he'd never make a scene where cell phones could start filming. "That's a sweet offer, princess. But you are absolutely not my type."

———

As soon as he's gone, we flee. Neither one of us can focus, and I'm so mad I want to destroy something.

"That asshole was my first kiss." I kick a pile of rotten dogwood blossoms. "Not that it was this precious flower I can never give away again or anything, but for the rest of my life, when people tell first-kiss stories, I'll have to think about Phillip Fucking Russell. *Around the frat house.*" Jess is quiet, so I keep going. "Did you notice how he called them his brothers?! Like, I get that it's a fraternity, so they're 'brothers' or whatever, but they're not. They're not family. They're a group of misogynist meatheads thrown together by patriarchy and . . . and privilege, and—"

Jess isn't beside me anymore. I stop and turn to see them frozen on the sidewalk.

"Jess?"

I rush back when they don't respond. They're standing there, trembling, as shaken as I am pissed. I take their hand and hold it steady. "Hey. Is this okay?"

They manage a nod.

"I'm not going anywhere."

I don't. We stand there, hands clasped. I'm such a selfish asshole, focusing on myself when Jess just got misgendered.

"I'm so sorry."

Jess gives a tight shake of their head. "Not here."

We don't say another word all the way back to my house. Inside, they curl up with the quilt on our beat-up couch and cup the tea I bring them, hands finally steady enough to hold it without spilling.

"Phil's your typical asshole jock. Trying to get a reaction. He wasn't really threatening me." I don't think. "But what he said to you—"

"It happens."

"It's not okay."

"I know that."

Of course they know that. A million times better than I do. As awful as it can be to be a girl in this world, people talk about it. There are hashtags and movements and marches. They don't always amount to action, but at least there are people who'll listen and relate and commiserate if I speak out, if Nor tells her story, and that's not nothing.

But for Jess, for others whose stories get swept into the darkest corners—they have more in common with Marguerite than I've thought about. And that's on me.

They're silent for a long time. Finally: "When I was in fourth grade, I spent months making this replica sword for a social studies project. I got special permission and everything, because weapons and school, you know?"

I curl up on the other end of the couch and tuck my toes under the quilt.

"I made the hilt out of clay, so I could do all these really cool, intricate carvings in them, and when I glazed it, it looked really cool. The blade was foam covered in aluminum foil. It wasn't the best part. But the hilt . . ."

My stomach twists. I know where this is going. Sweet little Jess makes this precious thing and then some douche-canoe like Phil Russell destroys it on the bus.

"Some kids might not have been allowed to keep their toy sword with them, but I was a good kid, right? Perfect grades, perfect attendance. I usually spent lunch reading. So my teacher let me take my sword with me."

I want to shield baby Jess from what's coming. I also kinda want to smack this teacher. How could they not see what would happen? Teachers, with their big hearts all thinking kids are good and pure or whatever, are clearly idiots.

"This one kid, Skylar Pressman—I still remember exactly where he sat on the bus because he and his junior dudebro friends always saved their straws from lunch and shot spitballs at anyone who wasn't them, so trying to avoid the line of fire was a strategic, stressful part of bus rides. But that day at lunch, Skylar stopped and asked if he could see my sword and I didn't want to hand it over, because he was Skylar Pressman, but also I had to because he was Skylar Pressman. He looked at it really carefully, like really examined it, and then he handed it back to me and said, 'Dude, that's sweet.' I never got hit by a spitball again."

I wait, to see if there's more. Like, I'm expecting Skylar Pressman to ambush them on the bus on the way home and steal the sword or something. Finally, I say, "I guess not all boys are monsters?"

"No, Skylar Pressman definitely was. His parents sent him to military school after he set fire to the girls' locker room in middle school."

I laugh. I can't help it. It's too predictable. "Do you still have the sword?"

"Oh, well. A few months later this new girl moved in across the street? Do you know Rajani Agarwal? She's on the swim team."

I try to place her, but can't.

"I saw her out in front of our house, and this other neighborhood kid was chasing her with something gross on a stick, I don't even know, like dog poop or a squashed slug or something, and I was overcome by a fit of chivalry—"

"Oh no . . ."

"Oh yes, so I grabbed my sword, which I had hung on my wall because I was so proud of it, and I ran out knowing full well the blade was foam, but hoping it would look impressive. I ran up to them, and without missing a beat, Rajani grabbed the sword from me, neatly disarmed the other kid, shoved the sword back at me, and said, 'I didn't need saving.'"

I need to figure out who Rajani is and become her best friend immediately. "Do you still have it?"

"Yeah, no. After Rajani went back in her house, the other kid grabbed the sword and destroyed it." Jess stares into the remains of their tea, like they'll find an answer there. "I wish I still had that sword."

I wish Jess had that sword.

I wish I had one of my own. Nor and Rajani too. That swords were something granted to us at a certain milestone, like tampons and puberty, and we were taught to use them, responsibly and with honor, that chivalry was an actual thing, not in the damsels in distress sense, but in the sense that we look out for one another and sometimes you might need my sword and sometimes I might need your sword, but we're never standing alone in the middle of a battlefield, defenseless.

LARDER MOUSE

E MUST GO TO SALETTE.

No one looks up.
The young master
has appeared then vanished
like so many times before
but now they feel his absence
in their open wounds
in the creak of the castle.
The stones will forget.
We women will not.

Ladies!

I summon Mother
when she instructs
the staff before a feast.

Betsy and Matilde
make no move,
but the younger ones
turn glassy eyes my way.

Gather cloaks and provisions—
only what we can carry.
We must reach
the convent by dusk.

Dawn is breaking.
On my own I could
make the trip in a day.

Weighed down
with so many others?
I'm not sure
we'll make it

at all.

THE WOMEN DON'T ARGUE
nor move with any speed.
I am glad of a task. In motion
I barely notice the blood.

I send the young ones
to check the stables,
saddle any horses
the soldiers haven't stolen.
If there is one bit of grace
there'll be a nag
to carry old Matilde.

Betsy and Zahra
will find makeshift cloaks
in blankets, table linens
anything to keep us warm.
Whatever they find
in these quarters below
for I will not send them
to the morgue upstairs.

That leaves me
to find provisions.

ZAHRA POINTS ME TO THE LARDER.
I push through a heavy door
then down a flight of stairs
to yet another door.

Who knew we kept our vegetables
and salted meats so well protected?

The room beyond the door is dark
and cool. It ought to frighten me
and yet there's something in this place
that feels like safety. I hear
the voice before my eyes adjust.

> *Your sister.*
> *Your sister has come!*

THE VOICE BELONGS
to a kitchen girl armed
with a fire iron
and a ferocious gaze.

Your sister, she said.
Your sister has come.

But that must mean—

I push past the girl
and find behind her
folded into almost nothing
my sister. Alive. Helene.

> *She doesn't want to be touched,*
> the girl insists.

Helene, I'm here.

She's silent
and still as stone.
I clutch my sister
to my breast,
feel her heart race
in time with mine.

The girl hovers,
grip still fierce
on her makeshift weapon.

I'm here, love.

I cannot say

it will be all right.

It won't.

EMILDE IS MY SISTER'S
champion. I didn't ask
her name but she informed me
as we carried Helene
up to the kitchen.

Young mistress!

Betsy wraps Helene
in the warmest blanket
they've found.

Oh, thank the saints.
Our little larder mouse!

Larder mouse!
She is the eldest daughter
of this estate, nobility
they serve. And yet—

Zahra tugs me aside.

She means no harm.
Your sister is wont to
hide away from parties,
revelry, inside the larder
with her books.

A seed of hope unfurls—
perhaps she was in the larder
the entire time. Perhaps
she never knew the horror.

But there has been no revelry here.
And my sister's silence shrivels
the seed before it can take root.

CHAPTER THIRTEEN

Around the frat house.

For once Jess isn't sprawled on my beanbag chair or my bed and I'm glad to be alone now that I'm the one shaking, heart pounding, falling apart.

I'd been sitting there in a coffee shop, doing something important to me, hanging out with a friend, working on my story, and that asshole thought he had the right to flip the tables. On me and on Jess. And the thing is, he does have the right. He was born into it. There are never any consequences.

There need to be consequences. Not only for Craig, but for Phil with his threats and entitlement, and all the football players and fraternity brothers, fans and alumni who rallied to defend a monster. Not because he was like them—scholarship water boy who didn't even get into a frat. But because they're like him. If it was criminal to take what you want from a girl, there wouldn't even be a football team. A Greek system. A university.

How many girls on that campus are now afraid of what would happen to them if they spoke up? If they stood up for Nor? If they told their own stories? They have stories. This was a heinous thing, but also it happens constantly.

And not just girls. Anyone with less power, representation. The ones who are overlooked, shouted down on the most basic things—why would they risk speaking up when they know how that turns out, even for the privileged?

I could have written survivor profiles until the end of time, if I wanted to. If they'd made any difference.

The ones who stay quiet, thinking about speaking up, have seen what happened to Nor and now they'll never speak. So the ones with power keep doing whatever they want. And the cycle continues.

Survivors need to know someone is in their corner. They aren't alone. Football players don't have all the power. Frat boys don't have all the power. Or they shouldn't anyway. And the only way to change that is to change that.

I grab my phone, scroll through several Husky hashtags for inspiration.

It's so obvious I almost laugh. These dawgs deserve to be shamed. I compose a Tweet.

> *Everyone's so quick to blame the victim, but maybe we should do some #DawgShaming. Craig Lawrence isn't the only rabid predator at UW.*

I look at it, knowing it'll bring some trolls to my account, but hopefully it'll get people talking. Survivors can share their stories. Predators will feel what it's like to have no control. Of course, only my followers will see it. I built up some platform throughout the trial with everything I posted, but those are mostly people who are already on Nor's side. I have to reach the others, the ones who are hiding, alone, the ones who most need a sword.

If I'm honest? I want to reach Craig's supporters too.

My muscles finally unwind, like I needed to get this out, and now that I have, my body melts into the mattress. I add #PurpleReign and #GoHuskies and click Tweet.

———

The knock on my door the next morning is too insistent to be either of my parents. They'd come in if they really needed to wake me up.

"What?" I call, squinting against the light that means the makeshift blackout curtain I put up to keep out news cameras has fallen down again.

"It's Jess. Are you decent?"

Jess always texts first. And never before noon. I don't know what time it is, but it's not noon.

"Yeah?"

The door bursts open and in an instant, Jess is on my bed, their phone in my face. "I am not sure you thought this all the way through," they say.

I sit up and grope for my phone on the nightstand. My notifications are out of control. Texts, DMs, Twitter mentions. I feel a little dizzy. I've written a few pieces that got a lot of attention. Not viral, per se, but shared by enough people with big platforms to make my notifications erupt.

Those were a fifth-grade science-fair eruption. This is Mount St. Helens.

"What is going on?"

"Does #DawgShaming ring a bell?"

Then I'm awake. My hashtag caught fire. This is what I wanted—attention on the issue, on the injustice. Light shining on the dark, festering places.

I scan through the hashtag. I see what I hoped to see—survivors opening up about their experiences. Some at UW, some at other universities and high schools. They're not naming names, but I get it. That's scary.

It's all good, though, because the more open people are, the less stigma for victims, the more consequences for perpetrators.

Every now and then some (white, male) rando is in my mentions, calling me a bitch or a cunt.

Cunt: a word for "vagina" that originally appeared in anatomy texts as a clinical term. Only later did it become obscene; in 1785 it was defined as "a nasty name for a nasty thing" in Francis Grose's *A Classical Dictionary of the Vulgar Tongue*.

But I've seen worse on the internet. It's worth it to open up the conversation. So why does Jess's face look like that?

"This is what I wanted," I try to explain. "Openness, discussion. I don't care if I get called a few names."

Jess types something into their phone and shoves it at me. "Do you care if Nor gets dragged into it?"

My stomach flips.

There's the familiar hashtag—#IgNorTheWhore—but there's a new spin on it.

Obviously we can't #IgNorTheWhore—she's like an STI that keeps coming back! So I say we send her #ToTheDawghouse!! #PurpleReign

They go on like that, blurring into one another, piling into a tangled heap, all focused on punishing Nor, making her pay, turning what I thought was so clever, so thought-provoking, right back around so it terrorizes the victim yet again.

Only this time it's definitely my fault.

———

"Sentáte, mija," Papi says with a firm pat on my shoulder. "I'll make some tea."

I sit. Tea isn't going to fix this. But at least he's doing something, instead of scrolling endlessly through Twitter, like Mom.

"I don't understand," she says. "Why would you do this?"

"I was trying to help!"

"How does this help? Who does it help? Not Nor."

"All the girls in this situation! This isn't only about Nor, you know! We can't just move on now that we got a guilty verdict and go, oh, that was justice! Because the sentence wasn't justice! Not even a little bit."

"Getting to trial was more justice than most victims see," Mom says.

"And that's supposed to be enough?"

"You take the win you get and you have a little gratitude! Nor is alive. We could have lost her. So yes! It's enough that I still have both my daughters."

"Well it's not enough for me." I'm on my feet. "But you just keep teaching fucking F. Scott Fitzgerald and Hemingway and whatever other goddamn toxic male shit you teach to reinforce this idea that boys are entitled to whatever the fuck they want!"

"Marianne," Papi says.

"Don't bother." Mom takes her phone and flees to the bedroom.

I collapse at the table and drop my head to its cool surface. I feel like I should cry, but mostly I still want to scream. I want to rage and hurt someone, even if that someone is my own mother who's done the best she knows how to keep our family together over the last year. Even her. Because everything she's done? It hasn't been enough. It hasn't been enough for Nor. It hasn't been enough for me.

Papi sits next to me, but I don't look up. He strokes my hair.

I used to get these terrible tangles, and when my mom would try to brush them out, I'd throw fits and jerk my head away and generally be impossible. Finally she threw her hands up and said fine, look like a feral child, I don't care. And I did, for a few weeks. Until I got tired of the matted hair and the looks from teachers and as a final straw, Zach Stein called me pube-head.

I wasn't about to go back to my mom and admit that. So I went to Papi, working on a leak in our kitchen sink, his tools spread all over the linoleum. I brought my sparkly purple hairbrush and asked him to help.

He used to do his sisters' hair, he told me later. When his mom got sick and couldn't anymore. His friends saw him once, braiding the little girls' hair and never let him forget it.

I didn't know that then. All I knew was Papi wouldn't need to talk about it. He would clear a spot for me on the floor and get to work. It was rough going. He got out a jar of coconut oil to help work through the tangles, but it was still a spectacular mess. Most parents would have given up. Better to haul the ornery kid to a salon and chop it off.

But I'd asked my dad for help and he was going to help me. We sat there together—it felt like hours—working at the knots, undoing what I'd done. Mom didn't say a word the next time she saw my smooth, sleek hair. Who knows what happened behind closed doors. After that, my dad was the only one who ever did my hair. French braids, fishtails, big poufy bangs for '80s day.

His touch on my hair is what undoes me now.

I only wanted to fix this but I'm making it worse. I'm a four-year-old with a hammer, trying to be Daddy's assistant, destroying the intricate dollhouse he'd spent months building for Nor. Only this time it wasn't a dollhouse.

Papi keeps stroking my hair until I finally stop sobbing.

"You need to apologize to your mother."

"I know." I hiccup. "How do I keep hurting everyone so badly when all I want to do is help?"

Papi covers my hands with his callused ones. "Creo que . . . we're figuring this out as we go along. For the longest time I felt completely frozen. I knew if I let myself do anything, it would most definitely make things worse for Nor. Para todos nosotros."

"How do you keep from storming the frat house with an AK-47?"

He passes a weary hand over his permanent five o'clock shadow. "A completely developed cerebellum helps. Also fairly inflexible views on gun control. And the fact that as much as I want to destroy that pathetic waste of oxygen and everyone who stands behind him, I can't bring myself to put this family through any more than we've already endured."

If I had more self-control. If I thought before I acted. If—

"When I met tu mamá, we were going to change the world with words. Me with poesía, her with novels. Grad school was this bubble where everyone believed words would be enough to save us all. But we got out and figured out words weren't even enough to pay the rent. Forget saving the world. The thing was, I was okay with that. I realized I could still write for myself, I could still read and enjoy poetry. I could learn a trade that would support a family. It was enough for me. Es suficiente para mi.

"Pero mija, my lovely, headstrong Marianne, you act because to do nothing would crush you. I don't think that will ever change. Espero que no. You won't be satisfied by enough, and you shouldn't be. You're going to fail spectacularly in your life. You are going to crash and burn, mi vida, pero, ay dios, what you'll make of the ashes."

His eyes fill with tears and he doesn't try to hide them. He holds my gaze for a moment, then stands and kisses the top of my head. "I'm going to check on tu mamá."

WIDE-OPEN NIGHT

O YOU KNOW
how to reach
the convent?

Zahra insists on walking
through the wide-open night
at my side, despite
her obvious pain. Despite
the space behind Matilde
on Minuit, the horse
I learned to ride on
as a child.

She leans on my arm,
her weight a welcome
tether to the earth.

I believe
the convent
is south.

I am
almost sure
we're headed
that direction.

This I know:

      each step carries us
      farther away from the place
      we'll never truly leave.

TIMES I HAVE LEFT THE CASTLE:

To visit cousins
in Avignon.

To attend a wedding
in Anjou.

TIMES I HAVE LEFT THE CASTLE
without my father's escort:

SOME HOURS LATER
we enter a village.
The servants breathe
more easily in the world
they know but the walls
on either side close in on me
with only room for the stench
the waste, the mangled creature
rotting in the road.

At any turn a man
could ambush us.
I force down
panicked breaths.

Mademoiselle?

I do not answer Zahra.
I cannot explain.
She slips her hand in mine
and I don't let go.

I WAS NOT WRONG
to fear
how men
would use
the shadows.

A woman's shout
slices the night.
I slip from
Zahra's grasp.

I am through
with cowering
as though each one of us
has not the strength
of all these men combined.

THE WOMAN'S SHOUT
is rage and fear
a rusty dull-edged blade
thrust deep as it will go
in desperate hope.

I do not see her
but she's there
behind the

> hulking shoulders
> one arm pinning
> prey against a wall
> the other unsheathing
> a weapon.

My first thought:

> You're one of Chalon's men.

Will that forever
be my impulse
when I see a man
with legs spread wide
entitled to the world?

ONE OF THE MEN
who slaughtered my family

or one who died defending us,
it doesn't even matter.

You flaunt your power
for no other reason
except your terror,
your fear that you are nothing
to this woman, to this world.

You're right to be afraid.

A LENGTH OF DISCARDED WOOD
in the alley, once a broom
or shovel or child's toy

is far from the weapons
Father trained me on
but you are not worthy
to die by my sword.

There will be no
parry and riposte,
no holding back
no decency.

There is no code of conduct here
only this weapon I've fashioned
from my rage and your fear.

THE WOOD IS SOLID, HEAVY
in my hands but lighter than
my brother's sword, the one
I practice with in stolen moments.

If there were time
I'd wonder if I'm capable.
I'd wonder if a sword feels different
when it meets with human flesh,
how the pain inflicted travels
through the weapon and back
upon the one who wields it.

There isn't time.

THE CRACK
of wood on a skull
strikes a triad chord.

One note: relief I hit my mark

Another: terror you'll turn on me

The third, the root: complete revulsion
at the thrill of what I've done
and how readily I'll do it again.

YOUR STUMBLE BACKWARD
was my aim; the woman's escape
exactly what I wanted.

Now I revel in your confusion—
expecting incensed brother, father,
and seeing instead a girl
with nothing for a weapon but rage
that's been sharpened against the stone
of a world that hates her.

YOU BITCH!

No time for technique; I react
on impulse to the tense of your muscles
the moment before you lunge,
surging forward, shoving you
against the wall with weapon
at your throat, roles reversed

       (how does it feel to be
       pinned and helpless?)

your face the face of every man
who terrorized my sister, my friend
the ones I love
            and me.

What if our bodies
are not for you?
What if you're not
entitled to the world?

THE TERROR IN YOUR EYES
is sweet in my soul.

I won't say I have no fear.
The difference between us is

I've nothing left
to lose.

YOU GASP FOR AIR
as I shove harder
against your throat.
It would only take
the last bit of my strength
to cut off your breath
and watch you die.

I could do it.

Right up until
I can't. I step back.
Your hands fly
to your neck,
your eyes fly
to meet mine.

There's a moment
where you consider
summoning
what strength remains
to show me exactly
how powerful you are.

But I'm not wrong—
you are a coward
fleeing into the darkness.

CHAPTER FOURTEEN

An uneasy peace settles on the house after Papi checks on Mom, after I apologize and she sobs and tells me she just wants it all to be over but she gets that it's not.

Mom leaves for an appointment. Papi leaves for a job.

Anytime I think about my Twitter feed the walls close in and I get a little dizzy, so finally I bury my phone in my closet and go to the backyard.

Chester follows me out. When I sit on the edge of the patio and wiggle my toes into the grass, he decides he doesn't have to keep such careful watch on me and ventures out to patrol the perimeter.

The Bianchis next door have a cat who lives to torment Chester. At least, that's how it looks from this side of the fence. When they first got the cat, it would sit on the other side and meow-scream at our poor dog. Chester dug under the fence until he made enough of a ditch that he could stick his snout under. Whereupon the cat would scratch his nose. Every time.

I don't know if Chester hoped there would be a different outcome each time he stuck his nose under there, or if he'd forget what had happened the last time, but he kept doing it until he got a scratch so bad it got infected and we ended up at the vet.

Papi covered the hole with wire mesh Chester can't dig through, but the vet told us to be vigilant, because Chester could try to dig another hole in a different part of the yard.

He doesn't look like he's scheming anything right now. But then you can't always tell by looking.

The familiar vocal patterns of NPR float over the fence on the other side of the yard, where Mr. Cho is probably working in his herb garden.

Somewhere in the distance kids shout. Chester cocks his head as a crow squawks overhead, landing on an electric wire and staring Chester down, daring him to bark.

A crow isn't worth Chester's time when his feline nemesis is clearly (but silently) taunting him from the Bianchis' yard. He stalks restlessly.

It's the kind of gloriously beautiful Seattle summer day that gets everyone out of doors, sends them in droves to Green Lake and Golden Gardens and Discovery Park.

My backyard will do for now. Toes in grass. A cat's meow. Chester giving up on the cat and coming over to rest his slobbery head in my lap. I can still turn this around. I can make this right.

I have the impulse to text Jess, or Francie and Sam, but I shake it off. No phone. Only me and creatures who will never understand the concept of a hashtag.

Chester pops up at the sound of the front door opening. Papi must have forgotten a tool. "I'm out here," I call.

Instead it's Nor who bangs the back door open. Chester is on her immediately but she doesn't even look at him. Instead she storms over as I'm getting to my feet and shoves me off the porch into the bushes below.

"Are you trying to ruin my life?!"

I barely feel the branches snagging on my skin, my flimsy T-shirt. I'm too stuck on Nor's rage. Her screaming. Nor has never screamed at me. She's never pushed me. Even as little kids, we weren't the kind of siblings who wrestled or roughhoused. Angry Nor withdraws, deploys the silent treatment with military-level precision.

Chester whips his head between us, unsure who's in more distress. I struggle to free myself from the branches. She stands there, red-faced, tears streaming down her cheeks.

"Nor—"

"No! No more talking from you! Can you shut your mouth for once? Stop all the words! The talking, the writing, the tweeting—"

"I am so—"

"Shut up! I told you stop! You're selfish and you're immature, but you're not stupid! You should be able to follow simple directions. You should realize this isn't a game! You don't get social justice points each time you pick up a megaphone! You destroy lives! I don't care if you're trying to help! Help who? You're only helping yourself feel like you're doing something, but instead you're making everything worse for me!"

She whirls around and stomps back inside.

Chester looks from the door to me. Then, with an apologetic glance, he follows her.

I don't know if I'm supposed to follow her. Part of me wants to, to defend myself, to scream back at her. But I also know she's not wrong, not entirely. Plus she made herself pretty clear about me keeping my mouth shut.

I go inside to get my phone. I have to text my dad, or Jess. Or even my mom. Francie or Sam. Someone to ground me in reality, remind me that we have not actually slipped into an alternate universe, despite all signs to the contrary. I'm not even sure if Nor will be in the house, or if she came all the way over from the U District to shove me into a bush and now she's on her way back, mission accomplished.

But on my way through the house to my room, I see, instead of Nor's battered car, a small U-Haul parked out front. Then I turn to see Nor coming down the hallway, hauling her desk chair.

"Move," she says, not even meeting my eye.

I step into the doorway of the bathroom so she can pass, and she takes the chair outside, puts it into the back of the U-Haul and comes back in.

"What are you doing?"

She pushes past me into her room, where she tries to pick up her desk and ends up hunched over with what looks like back pain. She lets out a huff and grabs her nightstand instead. Even that makes her wince.

"Nor, I can help you, but tell me what you're doing!"

"No more help from you." Not screaming anymore, but still shooting to kill with her laser eyes.

I go dig my phone out of hiding and text Jess and my dad both, telling them what's happening, telling them to get over here.

"Then Papi can help you. Or Jess. You're going to hurt yourself," I say when she comes back in from putting the nightstand in the U-Haul.

She stops at the hall closet and pulls sheets and towels out, pillows and blankets. "How about these?" she snaps. "Am I allowed to lift these?"

I sigh, going into her room and grabbing her laundry hamper.

"What are you doing? Don't touch my stuff."

"I thought you could put the linens in here."

She huffs again, then shoves the pile into the hamper with so much force I almost drop it. She grabs it from me and turns back toward the front door.

I open it for her and follow her out to the truck.

"Did you . . . move out of the dorm?"

She snorts and heads back to the house. "Moved, driven out by an angry mob with pitchforks and torches, whatever."

A vise squeezes my heart.

All those hashtag threats to send her to the doghouse . . .

I want to say something, anything. I want to take it back, but I can't. Right now, all I can do is help her fill up a U-Haul parked in front of our house, our home, where she could have moved if she was driven out of her dorm. But instead she's packing to go somewhere else.

The hamper in the truck, she sits on the edge to rest, her cheeks rosy from effort or anger. It feels like an offering, that she stays instead of running inside and slamming the door in my face. I sit next to her, ignoring the curious stares of Mr. Rawson and his Chihuahua as they walk by.

"Nor," I say. Almost in a whisper. "What happened?"

She doesn't answer for a while. But she doesn't yell or shove me off the truck, either. Finally, "It's not all your fault. It had been happening all along. Through the trial, especially after Douglas got behind him."

Matt Douglas, star Husky quarterback, who I guarantee had never once spoken to the water boy before, when asked by journalists about Craig Lawrence's character: "He always seemed like a really good dude to me. He's part of the Husky family."

"But it got a lot worse after you posted the hashtag." Nor puts a hand up to stop me before I can say anything. "I thought I could handle it. I did handle it. But then the door to my dorm room . . ."

I thought I'd already seen the depravity these assholes would sink to, but they went directly to where she lives?

"What did they do."

"You don't want to know."

"I really do. If you have to experience this, Nor, I can handle hearing about it. Especially when it's my fault."

"Partly your fault," she corrects.

It stings. As bad as I feel, as responsible and guilty, a part of me wants her to absolve me completely. To tell me it's not my fault at all, the responsibility lies entirely with Craig, with the Greek system, the football team, the administration, the fans, the world that hates girls.

"It looked like blood."

My head whips up.

"What they wrote on my door. It wasn't blood, but, like, it could have been. They wrote, *I know how to use a sword, cunt.* And they'd stuck a dagger sort of thing in the door."

"Oh my god."

"I didn't want to let them win. But I'm so tired of fighting."

I put a careful arm around her and she lets me, her head dropping down onto my shoulder. "They're monsters. And you shouldn't have to fight them alone."

She stays a moment longer, then lowers herself gingerly off the end of the truck. "I shouldn't have to fight them at all, but here we are. Help me with the desk?"

"The desk?" I follow her into the house. "How about lunch? We have lots of leftovers."

"I'm renting the truck by the hour," she says, going straight for her room.

The nightstand is one thing. No one cares about towels. But Grandpa built that desk for Mom when she started college. They couldn't afford for her to live in the dorm, but Grandpa wanted her to have a serious place to work. I've always been jealous Nor had it in her room.

"Where are you even going?" *Stay here,* I want to shout.

"These people from my gender studies class, they have an off-campus apartment with a room open for the summer. I want my desk there."

It's not her desk.

I leave her to pack up our family heirlooms and disappear to the kitchen. Will Nor ever cook here again, talking and laughing and whipping up something out of nothing? That's dramatic, maybe, but shit has gotten pretty dramatic around here. I open the fridge and stare. I'm not even hungry.

When I check my phone, both Papi and Jess have responded.

Papi's confused. Jess writes: "Heading to a longsword class. Will come over as soon as it's done. Unless you need me sooner."

That was twenty minutes ago, so by now they're dueling with some other medieval combat enthusiast. I'm still on my own.

I drape myself over the counter and rest my head on the cool surface. It smells like lemons.

"Are you going to help me?" Nor says from the doorway. "I can't do the desk on my own."

Now she wants my help. So she can take Grandpa's desk and run to people she barely knows. "You seem pretty determined to do everything else on your own," I snap. I pull out a jar of peanut butter, purely because I know Nor hates the smell.

"And you seem pretty determined to help me! That's what you call it, right? Helping? By getting me kicked out of my dorm?"

"You said it wasn't my fault!"

"I said it wasn't *all* your fault. So if you truly want to help, you need to stay out of every single thing to do with what happened to me."

"You know what? This didn't only happen to you!"

"Yes, it fucking did!"

Then why do I feel that dagger through her door in my own chest?

SWORD AND BOOK

 Y CHEST IS TIGHT
as we head into the mountains.

One thing on top of another
the siege, the alley
and no time to breathe
to stop and feel the weight.

We have a bearing now
and must proceed
if we're to reach the convent by dark.
The woman from the alley
directed us with longing,
held back from joining us
only by the children
hanging from her skirts.

AT THE CONVENT
women are betrothed
to Christ.

Tedious, a life of chants
and prayers, monotony
but also

Christ would not
slip into bed
demand his urges
fulfilled no matter

       the names he's called you
       times he's struck you
       your bone-deep weariness
       desperate longing to escape
       it all in sleep.

It's something
to consider.

WE REACH SALETTE
long after I've decided
I can't take another step.
And yet I do.

At the sight of our dismal group
the abbess at the gate
throws the doors open wide
metal on metal screaming our arrival.

        (battering ram on portcullis
        swords clash outside my door
        armor jostles as my chambers
        fill with men)

Zahra's hand on my back
anchors me to this moment
but my heart pounds
like I never left.

        (I never will)

Our infirm entrusted
to the care of the sisters
        (blessed art thou amongst women)
I volunteer
to guide the horses
to their own refuge,
reveling in a moment
free of responsibility
for all these other souls.

Zahra moves to join me
but I nudge her toward Helene.

Stay with her, please.

FOREHEAD TO MUZZLE
I breathe in the stable's
familiarity: hay,
sweat, safety.

But that's a story I tell myself.
We're no safer here than anywhere.
If those monsters could breach
a drawbridge and armed guards
how are rosaries and faith to stop them?

Child?

A novitiate
no older than myself.

Are you well?

I laugh.

My parents
are dead, my sister
mute with despair.

With every blink
I see behind my eyelids
the men who laughed
held me down
silenced me with filthy hands
took turns making a mockery
of every time I held a sword
and thought myself their equal.

I could do
with a bath.

LA SALETTES SANCTIFY THEMSELVES
with freezing water, no palace servants
to boil and haul the buckets that scald
their hands but warm my bath.

It doesn't matter.
There isn't water
hot enough to wash away
what's etched into my bones.

Even if there were
I've no desire
to linger, exposed
my body a living
history of horror.

IN A STARK ROOM
at a rustic table
Helene sits,
Zahra on one side
Emilde on the other
a crucifix behind them
and several hovering
angels in black.

A hunk of bread
tureen of pottage
sit untouched.

My stomach growls.

Where are the others?

Helene does not respond.

> *Some took to bed,*
> *some bathing.*

Zahra serves
a bowl of pottage,
pushes it my way.

Bed.
My muscles ache
but I'm loath to test
what will happen
when I close my eyes.

I push the bowl back toward Zahra.

Helene? Have you eaten?

Still no answer.

We've tried.

Emilde has never been more
than hands that brought my tea.
Would I have looked more closely
had I known she is my sister's
faithful shadow?

Are her parents dead like Zahra's?
(Like mine.)

Perhaps I should have thought
before I dragged these women
through the countryside
some might have kin, a warmer
comfort than these cold stone walls.
It's not as though their service
is required in my household any longer.

There is no household.

Two cots
fill a room
smaller than
Helene's larder.

No windows,
a single guttering flame
sends shadows dancing
across dingy walls.

Emilde settles
on a cot with Helene,
stroking her hair
humming in her ears.

I should be the one
to soothe my sister.
She should be the one
to soothe me.

But always we have been
brash Marguerite
ladylike Helene
in their own corners
with their sword
and their book.
Servants for confidantes
when all that time
there was a sister
who could have
should have
been there.

ZAHRA TUCKS IN BEHIND ME
shivering from the chill
or what we've survived
or both.

The pitch-black darkness
doesn't hide the fact
that four exhausted girls
have found a place
to lay their heads
but do not sleep.

No ice-cold water numbs me
no other bodies left to tend
my every muscle tenses
against intruders
brain races
but never fast enough
to outrun the images
sounds, smells
right there at fingertip
each bit of skin that touches
scratchy mattress is aflame
with other touches taking, desecrating.

HOURS LATER
breaths even out
advance retreat
the servants sleep.

Helene?

My sister lies
within my reach
and still I do not know
what she has suffered.

As though by knowing
I could change a thing.

CHAPTER FIFTEEN

Jess arrives before Papi to find me in the kitchen, eyes swollen, breath shuddery, hands covered in dough. They don't bat an eye; they throw on an apron and start helping.

When Papi bursts in, the first batch has just come out of the oven. "What's going on?" he says. "¿Y el U-Haul? Where's Nor? Are those . . . peanut butter cookies?"

"Indeed they are, Mr. Morales. Andrés." Jess glances at me and pushes a cookie on a napkin across the counter to my dad. "Nor's probably in her room. She's using the U-Haul to pack up some things she'll need in the off-campus apartment she's moving to."

Papi takes this in for a moment, then hurries down the hall. I grab the cookie and shove the whole thing in my mouth.

"You should try the longsword class with me," Jess says.

"Really?"

"What?"

"I should learn how to use a fucking sword?"

They blink, uncomprehending for a moment. "Oh, shit, no not because of that. For research on Marguerite. She's going to pick up a sword eventually, right? You've got to know how to describe that."

They have a point. But for all the words I've spilt, the idea of actually wielding a sword is terrifying.

"This is my decision!" Nor shouts from down the hall.

"Of course it is, morena! But I'll need to see if student housing can refund your dorm if we're going to afford an off-campus apartment."

"Someone literally stabbed a dagger through my door! You want me to stay there because you paid for it?!"

"¡No, mija, claro que no!"

"Then I don't really have a choice, do I?"

Of course she has a choice. She has a home, with a bedroom and a family and a dog. I could kind of understand when she wanted to stand her ground and show they couldn't run her off campus. But if she has to leave, why not run home?

She has a sister.

But maybe I'm why she can't be here. She's so pissed at me for everything I've done that she doesn't feel safe here, either.

Nor comes stomping down the hall, lugging a box of who knows what.

Jess lays a hand on my shoulder. A warning?

"You do have a choice!" I can't help myself. "This is your home. If you're so mad at me, then I'll go! I'll . . . stay with Jess for a while. I'll—"

Nor drops the box she was holding. Something inside breaks. "Oh my god, when are you going to realize this is not all about you? It's not about you at all!"

Chester noses his way between us, sticking closer to me. Nor may be red-faced and screaming, but my heart has stopped.

"Elinor." Papi stands behind her, careful not to touch her, but clearly aching to hold her. "No seas asi. She's trying to help."

Nor takes a steadying breath. She turns and faces Papi, completely unable to stand the sight of me. "The apartment I'm going to is free. Feminist pity or something, plus the room was already empty for the summer." She picks the box up off the ground and heads for the door. "And when you talk to the housing department, don't sign me up for a dorm in the fall."

CHAPTER SIXTEEN

Green Lake is at full capacity. Smack in the middle of Seattle, people stream around the three-mile route with strollers and kids, dogs and Rollerblades.

The path is barely passable on a day like this, but some sort of social order is maintained as serious runners and people on wheels stay to one side and everyone else stays to the other. But I can't deal with the paths. I can't deal with the dudebro runners who think because they bought some pricey spandex they suddenly qualify for the Olympics and all must clear the path to let them through. I can't deal with the yappy dogs whose owners insist they're friendly right up until they try to tear Chester's face off. I can't even deal with the babies in strollers, all adorable and innocent and completely unaware of how this world will destroy them in a few short years.

Instead, Chester and I sit close to the edge of the lake, but far away from the snack bar and paddleboat rentals and swimming area, with their happy families and splashing children and (potentially) people I know.

I thought being outside might help, since I can't write at home and now I'm paranoid in coffee shops. It takes Chester a while to understand that we're not going to walk or toss a ball. Finally he settles onto the blanket next to me, gazing forlornly out at the ducks in the middle of the lake.

I flip open the notebook and find some new illuminations. Jess adds to them whenever I leave it lying around. Sometimes I watch while they draw, but they get self-conscious and stop drawing, so I usually try to wait until they leave it lying around again. It's a game we're playing with each other.

I've finally tuned out the background noise and gotten into a groove when something hits me in the back of the head, hard. Chester jumps up, but instead of protecting me from an attacker, he grabs the weapon—a Frisbee—and goes running toward the water.

"Oh, shit, I'm so sorry."

Of course it's a dude, with no awareness of those around him. I sigh. If Chester hadn't run off with the Frisbee, I could have flung it into the lake and been done with it. If I turn around and see a UW T-shirt or any other collegiate attire, I may shove the perpetrator in the lake.

But he's wearing a GARFIELD HIGH DEBATE shirt, crooked glasses, and an unfortunate sunburn across his very fair nose and cheeks. He looks like he should be starring in a sitcom about a scrappy debate team captain who ends up in an R & J situation with the captain of the rival debate team. Except instead of double suicide, there's lots of biting sarcasm and dueling pop-culture references.

"My cousins are punishing me," he says, glancing nervously over his shoulder. "I basically destroyed them during a dinner-table politics conversation last night. So they're destroying me via Frisbee humiliation. Not that any of that's your problem. Any thoughts on how to get the Frisbee back from your dog, though? If it were up to me, I'd say the Fates had made themselves pretty clear and leave it to decompose at the bottom of the lake within a few millennia. But my cousins are pretty attached to their Frisbees. It's like an obsession. They call it disc golf? Have you ever heard of that?"

I'm supposed to find him charming, in this sitcom scene I've been thrust into. The earnest, babbling nerd who never has to worry about talking too much because that is not A Thing boys get accused of. The more they talk, the more charmed girls are. (Girls written by all-male TV staffs, that is.)

I blink at him, then turn to look out into the lake, where Chester is now gleefully treading water, gripping the Frisbee triumphantly between his teeth. "Chester! Come!" Chester absolutely does not come. And I will not be charmed.

"Baxter, come on!" a preppy-looking redhead whines from across the grass. "You better get that disc back!"

"Meet my cousin Darlene." Baxter—I guess—rolls his eyes. "Visiting from California."

I clap my hands. "Mr. Rochester, you come here now!"

"English lit fan?"

Here's where we bond over our mutually nerdy interests. "My sister named him."

"Ah." He sits down on my blanket.

"Uh. Make yourself comfortable?"

He scrambles up. "Oh, sorry. I thought we were talking."

Because a conversation I didn't even initiate is an invitation to go full meet-cute on me.

Did Craig attempt a meet-cute with Nor? Did he attempt fumbling-yet-adorable, and when that failed, resort to force?

"Am I gonna have to wade out there?" Baxter asks.

I shrug.

"He'll come back in eventually, right? He won't tread out there until he exhausts himself and drowns? I wouldn't sleep very well if I knew I was responsible for the death of Mr. Rochester. Even if he was a pervy creep. The guy from the book, not your dog. I don't know your dog."

It's the tipping point in the meet-cute scene—our shared aversion to Mr. Rochester. *You hate Mr. Rochester? OMG so do I!!!* The second I indicate we have a single thing in common, this guy will for sure expect my number and a date and who knows beyond that.

I'm not going to be cast in this role, and it's the only one available to me. I shove everything into my bag. "He'll follow me if he thinks I'm leaving." I walk briskly toward the path and sure enough, the moment I cross Chester's acceptable distance, he bounds out of the water and rushes to me, Frisbee in mouth.

I leash Chester, then toss the Frisbee back to Baxter. Or at least in his general direction. I might miss by a mile. "Sorry about that!"

Then I turn and get out of there before Baxter thinks we're friends. Or worse.

The familiar clanking of tools on pipes tells me Papi is finally working on our leaky sink. The cobbler's children will have shoes! Hopefully!

Except when I walk into the kitchen, the legs sticking out from under the sink are very distinctly not my dad's. Unless he lost fifty pounds and started wearing skinny jeans. And glitter Converse.

"Jess?"

Startled, they bash their head on the pipes—rookie mistake.

"Sorry, I'm so sorry!" I squat down to help them out.

"Everything okay?" comes Papi's voice from around the corner. "¡Ay, canchita! Don't scare my assistant! I haven't taught them the important art of emerging without a bash on the head!"

"Your . . . assistant?"

Jess grins and holds up a wrench. "Your dad was teaching me a few things."

"They've got a knack for it! More than you or Nor ever did." Papi grins and reaches out to ruffle my hair. With hands that have just been doing plumbing things.

I have no desire to join in, but also, Jess and Papi are bonding over plumbing. It feels like Papi and Nor in the kitchen, baking up something delicious while I sit around waiting to eat it.

"Are you guys hungry? I could make some sandwiches or something," I finally say.

But Papi's already eaten and Jess has to get to class.

"Sure you won't come with me?" Jess picks themselves up off the kitchen floor. "It's a drop-in class. You don't have to have previous experience or anything."

"Are you sure? I don't want to cramp your style with your medievalist friends."

Jess rolls their eyes and hands the wrench over to Papi. "Thanks for teaching me about pipes, Mr. Morales. I feel I have become a more productive member of society today."

Papi claps Jess on the shoulder. "It's Andrés, my friend. And barring a plumbing emergency, let's plan on Tuesday for some parallel-parking lessons, ¿sí?"

The longsword class is held in the basement of a Unitarian church in the U District, with a giant rainbow flag and a sign that says LOVE IS LOVE IS LOVE IS LOVE IS LOVE. Jess salutes the flag as we walk in, but then says, "The Unitarians are totally cute, but the class is an outside group. So FYI . . . not everyone here is training for the resistance."

I'm not an idiot. Any delusions I had that Seattle was some sort of liberal bastion of progressive, intersectional feminism was thoroughly squashed by the number of people more concerned about a distraction to the Husky football prospects than a woman's right to be safe in her body. But if I'm honest, I did kind of expect the class to be a group of people like Jess—medievalists, Ren Faire enthusiasts, LARP-ers. Theater kids all grown-up. If my assignment to cover entertainment for the *Oracle* my freshman year taught me anything, it's that theater kids *are* all training for the resistance.

Jess is right, though. When we walk into the dimly lit room, no one immediately jumps out as someone you'd pick for your trivia team because of their extensive Sondheim knowledge. A couple of young, heavily tattooed white women in expensive yoga clothes are having an intense conversation in one corner. A diverse trio of middle-aged men stretch in another corner, one wearing a SEAHAWKS T-shirt and another wearing a ratty shirt that says VISUALIZE WHIRLED PEAS.

A guy in his mid-twenties is standing too close to a beefy guy in a kilt who's unpacking equipment from storage bins.

"Come on, man," the young guy wheedles. "I'm ready. You've got to let me—"

"Nope." Kilt Guy isn't having it. He keeps putting a storage bin between them, but then Personal Space Guy moves around to get too close again. It's uncomfortable to watch. The other one could probably strangle him with one hand. From the look on his face, he might.

"I could be teaching this class! You're on such a power trip, dude—"

Kilt Guy shakes his head and walks away, continuing to set up.

Privilege: being able to turn one's back on an angry white dude without worrying about consequences.

"Okay, so this is an ongoing thing," Jess whispers. "Mack's the teacher"—they chin-point at Kilt Guy—"and honestly I don't know how he hasn't run that asshole through with a sword yet."

"What does the asshole want?"

"Isaac? He wants to learn super-advanced techniques no one here is anywhere near ready to use. Including him. He gets here early and stays late, just to fondle the swords." Jess waggles their perfect eyebrows at me.

"Hello." Suddenly Mack is in front of us. "Who's this? You bring a friend, Jess? Oh, and did you check out that book on mounted combat I told you about?"

"Yes, ohmigod!" Jess turns on their fanperson voice. "It was exactly what I needed to finish my cosplay. Thank you! This is Marianne."

I stick my hand out to shake. "Em."

"Any experience with swords, Em?"

"Uh, no."

"She's a writer. She's writing a book set in medieval France—"

I stop Jess before they bore this guy with the entire plot of my story. "I was hoping I could observe the class."

"Nope." Mack uses the same final tone he used with the asshole from before. "No one observes. You participate or you hit the road."

"Told you," Jess says.

"Circle up, warriors!"

Isaac the Overconfident is the first one to the circle, letting out a loud battle cry. He's ready to defend Seattle against the forces invading to . . . pillage our coffee? Lay siege to the Amazon Spheres?

Mack gives him a withering look. "Today we're going to work on a strike from above and a wrath strike." He points a sword at me. "You in or out?"

I feel like learning how to use a fucking sword.

"I'm in."

KNOW MY NAME

HE BELLS THAT BECKON
to morning prayers
do not awaken me;
I never slept.

Zahra stirs, peaceful
until her eyes open
and she remembers.
Her gaze falls on my face
as tears slip down her own.

I long to comfort her
for all the times she's
held my hand
dressed my wounds
scrubbed my stains

but there is comfort
in the roles we know.

She slips from bed,
retrieves the stack of garments
left by the door in the night
and sets two shapeless shifts
upon the bed where Helene lies
safe, wrapped in Emilde's arms.

We could stay here until
my brother returns.
Or if he doesn't, until
the horrors beyond these walls
fade. Or if they don't
perhaps we simply stay.

I CANNOT STAY HERE
with my softest parts
exposed.

Even the modest garments
provided by women
betrothed to Christ
cannot contain
cannot keep out
the ugliness.

I require
armor.

IF SOMEONE ELSE
should slay the monsters
it will be in the name
of land and power and wealth
not Marguerite de Bressieux.
Not in the name of Helene
or Zahra, Emilde, Betsy.

They must know our names.

AT BREAKFAST
I tell the women
who have given their lives
in servitude to my family
they are free to return
to their homes.

This pronouncement
is met with fear, tears.
They have nowhere to go.

RESTLESS, I WALK THE GROUNDS.

Through massive windows
morning light illuminates
the sisters, anonymous,
hunched over gilded pages.

Beyond the scriptorium,
the chapel, and then
a small stone outbuilding
jutting from its side.
A flash of movement
from within
catches my eye.

It could be any of the sisters
attending to their many tasks
but I'm reminded of the anchoress
Father told us of years ago.

Religious recluse walled into a cell
with no way out, not betrothed
to Christ, but divorced from the world.
Not imprisonment, but choice
to spend one's days in isolation, prayer.

Philippe had laughed.

A witch!

Father's rebuke
was instant.
Philippe's cheek flamed
where Father dealt the blow.

*The anchoress is
to be respected.*

Could the flash in the window
be the anchoress we learned of
all those years ago?
Still living out her days
with stones for company?

How long
can one endure
such solitude?

I draw nearer.
The opening in the wall
is less window than
slightest gap allowing
air and a glimpse of sky.

Perhaps exhaustion birthed
the movement, my brain
creating a world in which
a woman could choose
the life she wants.

There are no doors;
no one could ever
storm this castle.

I peek in the gap.

Blessings upon you, child.

SHE IS PERHAPS MY MOTHER'S AGE,
long hair tied back
shift loose upon her frame.

Blessings to you.

How does one greet a person
who's chosen isolation?
Have I intruded?

> *May I pray for you, my child?*

I stumble back.
I couldn't fathom it
when Father told us
but now I see why
she might choose a life
where no one can ever touch her.

BUT IF SHE WAS DRIVEN HERE BY FEAR,
doesn't she live with it every day,
the walls a constant reminder?
Or maybe fear is a constant
no matter the walls.

And did she truly choose it
or was it chosen for her by a man
she inconvenienced by existing?

So many questions but all I say is

I have to go.

154

I HAVE TO GO.

Even if
four walls of stone
could keep me safe

I cannot hide

while men
who gutted my life
so many lives

are free
to ravage
all of France.

THE SECOND NIGHT
the others sleep more quickly,
endless weight upon the scales
pressed down until there's no more give.

I drop a kiss on Zahra's head
and then Helene's. A silent thanks
to Emilde, my sister's constant
no matter my fate.

I slip out into the night.

THE CONVENT IS QUIET AND DARK
as I lead Minuit to the gate,
save for a flickering
at the anchoress's window.
Does she see me go?
Would she stop me
if she could?
Does she envy the freedom
of a girl with a horse
or has she found
the freedom she sought
in locking herself away
from the world of men?

THIS TIME I'M READY.
As I ease it open
the gate's protest
                    metal on metal
awakens not what's past
but what's to come.

CHAPTER SEVENTEEN

The apartment building is a long way from campus, with some sort of clinic on one side, sketchy-looking people camped out on the sidewalk, and a boarded-up building on the other. I can totally see why Nor would rather live here than with her family at home.

I clamp down on my inner snark. Nor reached out. She invited me over. I'm not going to screw this up.

I text to let her know I've arrived, since something crusty is growing on the buzzer panel, which looks like it hasn't been touched in about half a century anyway. The door clicks and I step inside.

It smells like weed and rat poison.

My breath starts coming faster. My palms are sweaty. I'm nervous—to see my sister. My best friend. I take in the slowest breath I can manage considering I feel like I'm about to be shoved into a coliseum to face some underfed, abused beast.

"Up here!" A head appears over the railing a few floors up. "I'm Tonika! Nor's roommate. Come on up!"

Roommates. I knew they existed, but I've been so focused on seeing Nor again that I didn't think about meeting her roommates.

Tonika pulls me in for a hug the moment I reach the third-floor landing. Then she pulls back and holds me at arm's length, like our great-aunt Phyllis does when we haven't seen her in a few years.

"You look so much like Nor!" she says. "She talks about you constantly. Come in! She's in the shower. She left her phone out for me to buzz you in if you texted."

We used to think it was funny, how sometimes growing up people didn't even believe we were sisters. I was always fair, with thin, light brown hair and light brown eyes. When we visited Guatemala, Papi's family would call me canchita and I was confused because Spanish class taught me that meant blond. I'm not blond.

Nor's always been darker, morena, especially in the summer, with thick, glossy waves of nearly black hair and eyes to match. The nicknames weren't good or bad, only facts, so commonplace and neutral to comment on appearance. Mom wasn't thrilled when they called her gordita, but Papi insisted it was loving. Most of his family members call him cabezón—big head—so all things considered, gordita wasn't bad.

Maybe because our tíos and tías and primos are all much more moreno than canche, I've always felt like Nor belongs with Papi's family in a way I don't and never will.

Tonika says we look alike, and we do, in our bone structure, the shape of our noses, our smiles. For someone passing by, though, we look worlds apart.

I follow Tonika into the apartment, which smells more like freshly baked chocolate chips cookies than the patchouli incense I was expecting. To be clear: The apartment is most certainly a shithole. But it's the shithole of poor college students using milk crates as end tables. They're not cooking meth.

Tonika knocks on the bathroom door as we pass it and hollers, "Your baby sister's here!"

She leads me into the living room–kitchen area, where chocolate chip cookies cool on the counter. "Help yourself," she says. "We forgive your sister for turning the oven on in this heat because she is a culinary goddess. Want something to drink? Too hot for coffee, though. Wyatt's home-brewed kombucha?"

I perch on a wobbly barstool and take a cookie. "Water would be great."

She laughs. "I don't blame you. He hasn't killed us yet, but it's always a gamble." She sets a glass of water in front of me. "You're a writer, yeah?"

I'm confused for a second. Nor doesn't even know about Marguerite.

"Nor says you're on the school paper?"

"Oh yeah. I was." Loud electronic music drifts through the ceiling from the apartment upstairs. There's a water stain on the ceiling that would give Papi a heart attack. "Who else lives here?"

"Right now? It's me and Nor and Wyatt. My girl, Lola, went to Puerto Rico for the summer, so Nor's in her room."

"Who's Wyatt?" When Nor said she was moving in with some people from her gender studies class, I'd assumed they were all women. Which was stupid of me, now that I think about it. It seems like lately I'm wrong about everything.

Tonika pulls a photo off the fridge and sets it in front of me. She's at a concert with a short, round Latinx girl on one side, and a super-tall, gangly white guy on the other. "Lola, and this here's Wyatt. I think he's working today."

The bathroom door opens and Nor comes out in the same faded green sweats she's had forever, looking almost like my sister. Her hair is all wrapped up in a sort of turban thing on her head. But I catch a glimpse of the Fremont High Eagle.

"Are you wearing my T-shirt on your head?"

She reaches up and touches the makeshift turban. "It cuts down on the frizz," she says. As she brings her hand down, I catch a glimpse of something on her wrist.

"Is that . . . did you get a tattoo?"

"Oh. Yeah." She holds it out, shy.

I don't grab her wrist the way I would have, before. Instead, I step closer and lean in to look. It's a tiny line drawing of a butterfly. I almost miss the fact that the body is a semicolon.

"She was very brave," Tonika says. "Except for the part where she was a total baby."

"Hey!"

Tonika laughs as her phone buzzes. She waves it at us and heads to her room.

Nor sits down with me and grabs a cookie. "What do you think? I'm playing with the recipe."

"They're good. Something's different. Sort of . . . herbal? Wait, these aren't—"

Nor laughs, finally a familiar thing in a world where Nor has a tattoo and roommates she trusted more than me to go with her. "They are not pot cookies. But good call on the herbal—they've got thyme."

For a second I think she means time. Like time is an ingredient we could bake into things, fold into the batter of our lives to give us the space we need to process and heal, move fluidly back to change things or forward to where the edges won't feel so sharp.

"They're really good. Can I take some home for Papi?"

"Sure." She narrows her eyes at me. "But they better make it home to Papi."

"I swear."

"I wanted to talk to you about Mom. Her birthday's next month."

"Okay."

"She turned fifty last year."

I take another cookie to hide my surprise. I probably should have known that. But I can't even remember her birthday last year. I can't remember mine. The trial prep, the postponements, the media, the continuances.

Reading my mind, Nor says to the counter, "We just completely skipped over it. It was right when . . ."

"Right."

"So I think we should do something special this year. To make up for the one we missed."

"Like a party?"

"Ew, no. I mean, with our family, sure. But more like a special gift from the two of us."

Lately I've spent all my money on longsword classes and obscure books about medieval warfare, but I can't tell Nor that. It feels like a secret, for some reason. Maybe I don't want anyone to think I'm actually training to avenge my sister.

"I was thinking like a scrapbook. We could gather old pictures and try to contact people she went to school with or whatever and get them to write cards. Make it pretty. It wouldn't have to cost much, but I think it would mean a lot to her."

"That would be nice."

"I know the last year has been kind of shitty for all of you and it's—"

"You better not say it's your fault."

She pauses. "You're right. It's not. But I don't want everything to be about me. I was terrible to you that day at the house, packing my stuff."

"Only that day?"

She gives me a gentle shove. Much gentler than when she literally shoved me off our porch into the hydrangea.

"I'm sorry. Okay? I know it hurt your feelings that I didn't move home. But being here is good for me. It gives me some space. Obviously being on campus was too toxic. And being at home feels too smothering. It's not you, it's Mom and Papi. They mean well, but they handle me like I'm made of spun glass."

She gets a text and glances at her phone. She laughs and holds it up. Mom, just checking in.

"I have to figure this out on my own. How to move forward. I have to control something. And this . . . being on my own, here, makes me feel like I am."

I can see that. "Tonika's really nice."

"She is! Wyatt is too. You'll meet him another time. He writes a column for the *Daily*."

I stare into my tea, hoping to avoid any conversation about journalism. "So is this where you're going to live in the fall?"

She sighs. "I wish. But Lola will come back and want her room. So it's kind of up in the air. I'm trying to take things one day at a time, you know?"

CHAPTER EIGHTEEN

No matter how sweltering our cramped main floor gets in the worst heat of summer, the basement is always a refuge. Stuffed to the ceiling in some corners with generations worth of stuff, sure, but that's what you get when you live in the house your mom grew up in.

It's ancient and tiny and falling apart, but there's history here.

On the absolute worst summer nights when Nor and I cursed our parents' refusal to get air-conditioning, I used to haul a pile of blankets down and sleep on the cool concrete. Nor would never come, though. She preferred to sweat it out in her suffocating bedroom rather than sleep with the shadows and ghosts.

One night my mom came down with her own blankets and slept with me. She told me she used to escape to the basement too when she was little. I thought maybe this would be our thing, like Papi and Nor had cooking together, summertime slumber parties, telling mother-daughter stories, really listening to each other without all the other stuff always getting in the way. But it happened only the once.

I've dragged some photo albums down to the basement from the living room—baby pictures and elementary school report cards. Nothing earlier than photos of my mom, pregnant with Nor. I pull out a few of those—my parents all young and fresh, Mom looking like she's playing a pregnant lady in a play, a basketball stuck up her dress.

Then they're both beaming and bleary-eyed in the hospital, staring at a bundle of Nor, my mother's hair stringy and plastered against her forehead, Papi hunching over the hospital bed, near collapse.

Mom was in labor with Nor for more than twenty-four hours. She'll tell you the bare minimum, if you ask, but when she does, she'll look so haunted you'll never ask again.

Papi remembers Nor's birth differently. Like some great athletic achievement, an Olympic triathlon, or climbing Mount Rainier. My birth story is the one that haunts him, but Mom will tell it over and over to anyone who'll listen.

They thought I would come slowly, since Nor had. So they weren't worried when labor started while they were hiking on the east side. Mom wasn't even convinced it was labor. Apparently I'd been torturing her—her word—with Braxton-Hicks contractions for weeks. Braxton-Hicks aren't true labor but are very real in their pain and intensity, which my mom will let you know if you do not already and maybe even if you do.

They took their time getting off the trail and back to the car, the better to help the labor along. Mom didn't want to spend another miserable twenty-four hours in the hospital if she could help it, so she planned to labor on her own as long as possible.

Toddler Nor was with them—I grab a photo of her in one of those baby backpacks, probably not from that day, but close enough—so they took the time to change her diaper and get her a snack before they began the drive back into Seattle.

As soon as they hit the highway, the labor started getting more intense. (At this point in the story, Mom will say, "Things were really progressing!" and Papi'll say with the look of a man who's done multiple tours of duty in a combat zone, "The screams . . . I'll never forget the screams . . . ")

Nor claims she remembers, but probably she's heard the story so many times it's burned into her brain. They had explained to her in toddler terms what happens during a birth, but they had been planning to have Uncle Joel babysit when they went to the hospital, so no one was quite prepared for labor in an enclosed space with a toddler present to scream along.

They were on the 520 Bridge, a mile-and-a-half-long bridge across Lake Washington, when my mother screamed at Papi to pull over because she could feel the head crowning. But it's this narrow bridge and there's not really a shoulder. It was rebuilt a few years ago, with nice walking paths and more space, but apparently when I was born, it was completely unsound, structurally, this bridge that actually floated on top of the water, and Papi tried to pull over the best he could, but really that meant he blocked a whole lane of traffic, so all these cars were honking and traffic was building up as they tried to get around him.

And it's a floating bridge, right? So this was a super-stormy day—at least, according to Papi's telling of it. My mom rolls her eyes when he gets to this part and says there were "light showers." But to Papi, the only thing dividing the choppy, black waves from his pregnant wife, their almost-born baby, their toddler, and the car they were all in was a flimsy traffic barrier.

At this point Papi always points out that he can't swim. "No one has backyard pools en la zona 18," he'd say. But I mean, if we all plunged over the side of the bridge in a gale force wind, I think we were pretty much toast even if he could swim.

Of course Papi called for an ambulance, but the traffic was all backed up because we were blocking a lane, so he didn't even know if an ambulance was going to be able to get through. All they had were those ancient flip phones, so he couldn't Google how to deliver a baby, meanwhile Nor was screaming her head off, so he dug around and grabbed a shirt from his soccer bag in the backseat—they still have the shirt, I swear to god—so he could be ready to swaddle me or whatever.

Mom swears Papi started freaking out then that they needed to boil water. Like, that's what they do in all the movies, right? And he was all "¡Agua hervida! How do we boil water? We're surrounded by water but it's not boiled!"

While he was freaking out about the lack of boiled water, which I'm pretty sure is for sterilizing instruments they didn't even have, Mom reached down and pulled me out. (I gather it's more complicated than that, but she makes it sound that easy.)

So there are no exhausted but happy pictures of them with me in the hospital. We did eventually get to a hospital, but everyone was sort of in triage mode at that point and I'm just lucky they remembered to pick me up from the nursery when they headed home.

That harried beginning set the tone, I guess, because there are only a fraction of the number of baby photos of me as there are of Nor. I get it, the novelty wears off. Keeping a baby and a toddler alive makes snapping a cute photo a lower priority.

Anyway.

It turns out keeping us alive was the easy part.

The basement is cool as always, and I know I'll find more photos down here, more history than the limited scrapbooks from upstairs. Mom did have a life before childbearing, after all. There's camping gear, an old trampoline, the collapsible clothesline thing that stays inside most of the year because line-drying in Seattle is kind of more aspirational than practical. Tools that never get used, holiday decorations, the DIY treadmill desk Mom sprained her ankle on the first time she used it.

I know there's a bin labeled PHOTOS near the holiday stuff, because I see it every year when Mom sends me to dig out the Christmas tree stand. It's buried under some fabric from back when Mom used to upcycle thrift store sheets into circle skirts and sundresses, very Maria von Trapp. I haul it out.

I sit down in a clear square of space with the bin, but inside, instead of a treasure trove of heartwarming family photos, I find some old baby clothes, random financial documents, and expired passports.

I grab the passports—the pages with Guatemala stamps could go in the scrapbook. But bank statements from before I was born, probably not.

If the bin labeled photos contained baby clothes, maybe the bin labeled baby clothes has photos? I haul the supposed baby clothes out from under a knockoff Barbie DreamHouse.

My impeccable logic delivers, sort of. There are no baby clothes inside. It mostly looks like paperwork, but more of a miscellaneous jumble than the financial stuff in the other bin. I settle in to sort through. A miscellaneous jumble could be promising.

A bunch of paperwork for Papi's immigration status, Mom's college transcripts, our vaccination records, some wedding photos—jackpot. My parents a million years ago, Mom with her hair long and curling around her shoulders, Papi clean-shaven, eyes bright. I set the best ones with the stack of usable items.

Some ancient zines and poetry chapbooks are another find from the baby clothes box. I decide not to bother with Mom's high school yearbooks. If I get desperate I could copy some pages, but I don't want to cut them up without permission.

The rest of the box is paper, and I'm about to pile everything I'm not taking back on top when a word catches my eye: Snowblood. I pull it out. It's not a single sheet, but the cover of a thick spiral-bound manuscript.

From Lady Snowblood to Kill Bill:
How the Ongoing Legacy of Male Filmmakers Perpetuates
the Male Gaze in Film Depictions of Female Vengeance

A DISSERTATION

SUBMITTED TO THE GRADUATE SCHOOL OF
COMPARATIVE LITERATURE, CINEMA & MEDIA

AND THE COMMITTEE ON GRADUATE STUDIES

OF THE UNIVERSITY OF WASHINGTON

IN PARTIAL FULFILLMENT OF THE REQUIREMENTS

FOR THE DEGREE OF

DOCTOR OF COMPARATIVE LITERATURE

Katherine Messer

January, 2002

A WIDER STANCE

STAY OFF MAIN ROADS
            a woman alone.
At least the convent's garments
are less likely to catch the eye.

But even in the habit
of the Mother Superior
the wrong man could
consider me prey.

My hazy plan
to find the monsters
and vanquish them
is hazier with every hoofbeat.

I only know
I cannot bear inaction.

CHILDHOOD DINNERS
with visiting nobles
were torture worse than
embroidery lessons.

Until, that is,
we received a visit
from the Duke of Anjou
and his wife.

Isabella of Lorraine
intrigued me because of
her age
        (older than her husband)
her education
        (raised to rule Lorraine)
her conversation
        (unconcerned with her role)

The duchess was also
unconcerned with my role.
Girls did not speak
at the dining table
and yet Isabella
directed questions to me.

Mother's eyes upon me,
I was in a quandary. After all
it would be ill-mannered
to ignore a guest.

The next night I was seated
far from the duchess
but I had been emboldened.

A taste of having my voice heard
and suddenly I wanted the whole pie.

Mother banished me
to dine in my room.
I snuck instead to the stables
to practice footwork
with my makeshift sword.

I jabbed and parried with a bale of hay
dropping the improvised weapon
when Isabella's voice cut
through the horse's whinnies.

Widen your stance, darling.

I whirled around, feet still close together
and toppled to the side. She laughed.

But it wasn't a laugh like Papa's
or Philippe's when I'd stumble.

Claim your space.
A wider stance
a stronger base.
Use the strength
in your entire body
not only your arm.

To my amazement
this noble lady, this duchess
lifted a hayfork and
spread her legs wide.

Though Father had taught me
the basics, I somehow believed
        my childish world revolving on my axis
myself the only girl in all the world
to ever lift a sword.

Isabella knew sword-fighting.
She said she must
for she loved her husband
very much and what if

        someday

he were taken from her
and she had to avenge
his honor?

ANJOU IS NOT SO FAR.
I think.

If Isabella and her husband
have escaped the raids
she will help me
discern what's next.
I hope.

Anjou is not so far
but Minuit must rest
as he is powered
by muscle and bone
and not a grief so pure
it could fuel me
to the ends of the earth
until my sword
sinks into the flesh
it seeks.

CHAPTER NINETEEN

I get to the church so early the doors are still locked. There's a man curled up in a sleeping bag on the landing, but he doesn't move a muscle when I knock. I wonder if he's so deeply asleep he doesn't hear me, or if he's learned to tune out whatever doesn't involve him.

I hope he's not dead.

No one answers the door and I don't want to keep pounding, in case I wake the man, so I settle on the bottom step and pull a book on medieval France out of my bag. I'm still trying to figure out the distance from Marguerite's home estate to Isabella's in Anjou, and how long it would take to travel by horseback.

"I know a lot about France," says a voice right over my shoulder.

I slam the book shut. At first I thought it was the sleeping-bag dude, but no, the mansplainer is none other than Isaac the Overconfident.

"Geez, jumpy. I was only trying to help."

I so don't want to deal with this guy, especially right now when there's no one else around. But precisely because of that, and because he has a passion for deadly weapons, I plaster on a careful smile. Not so friendly that he thinks I'm going home with him; but not so cold he decides I'm a frigid bitch.

"Thank you."

Apparently my smile wasn't warm enough.

"Yeah, you sound really grateful." He sits on the step right next to me. His sweatpants brush my leg. I want to move but I'm frozen and I'm pissed that I'm frozen because I'm not a delicate flower, I'm the kind of girl who gets up and moves if a guy makes her uncomfortable (aren't I?) but I shouldn't have to be any kind of girl; I should be able to sit here and wait for the doors to open without carefully weighing my every shift and breath to be sure I don't set off a brosplosive.

"I could be teaching this class, you know. Whatever you want to know about medieval warfare, I could tell you."

He smells nice, which pisses me off further. He should smell like corn chips and body odor and his mother's basement.

"What, you giving me the silent treatment?" His hair is flat and parted in the middle, like a washed-out Severus Snape, with none of Alan Rickman's appeal. "Are you one of those girls? Too good to talk to me?"

"No, I . . ." And again the rising fury that I can't respond how I want to respond, that I am absolutely too good for him, not because I'm any sort of girl, but because he is the sort of guy who feels entitled to every girl's perfect smile, perfect attention, perfect response to every unasked-for lecture. "I was just listening to you."

I hate myself. But that appeases him for a second. Behind us, the sleeping bag rustles.

"If you're serious about swordsmanship, you've got some work to do," Isaac says. "I was watching you last class."

That's enough to propel me off the step. No thought for whether he might breathe fire. I'm not sitting pressed up against him for another second. "I'm just doing some research," I say from a safer distance.

He nods. "You're not really built for swordsmanship anyway." He smirks. "Swordswomanship? You're top heavy, so your center of gravity is all wrong."

Top heavy. Suddenly all I can feel are my boobs. It's like the days right before my period starts when I'm so aware of my boobs with every step, like they enter a room before I do, shout their existence at me every second. Except right now it's all of that, but also there's nothing else. I am all boob.

"Here, I'll show you." He's on his feet, he's right in front of me, too close, he's reaching into his bag, there isn't even time to panic before he pulls out what turns out to be a collapsible umbrella.

I stumble back, which he takes as invitation to demonstrate his umbrella-wielding skills.

I glance around. It's a busy street. It's not like he's got me in some remote location. Not even like we're alone inside the building. Nothing's going to happen to me.

So why is my heart racing?

I could walk away. I could walk away and step inside the first shop, or strike up a conversation with a passerby, or run to catch the next bus that stops half a block from here.

But that seems more dangerous than staying. What happens the next time he sees me?

"You take it." He shoves the umbrella into my arms. I don't want it, but I take it, and my anger boils. "Show me your thrust."

I am not performing in the middle of the sidewalk for this asshole.

"You shy?"

He takes a step toward me and I thrust the umbrella into his gut. Instead of getting pissed though, he laughs. "Right, so you proved my point! Because when you tried to thrust, your . . . anatomy got in the way and I barely felt it."

My anatomy.

"Here, let me show you."

In an instant, he's behind me, arms pinning mine to my side as he reaches around to hold the umbrella, like in a rom-com when the girl's mini-golf date helps her improve her swing, but this is no rom-com and the blood is pounding in my head, and I struggle against his scrawny arms, which are much stronger than they should be.

"Get off me!"

"You want to learn, don't you?"

I struggle harder, he holds on tighter.

I catch a blur of movement on the church steps out of the corner of my eye and hope the instructor's arrived, but then Isaac howls and I'm suddenly free.

"You bitch!" he screams, but not at me, and from where I've staggered a few feet away, I turn to see not a guy after all, but a woman of indeterminate age, so weathered by whatever put her on the streets she could be twenty or sixty. She wields a box cutter and a steely gaze.

Isaac clutches his upper arm like he's got a grievous battle wound. "Cunt!"

She says nothing, but keeps her weapon ready.

His gaze turns on me, but then flips back to her. "Fucking cunts, both of you!" Then he turns and runs down the street.

The woman snorts, then moseys back up the steps to her nest of belongings on the church stoop.

"I . . . thank you."

She ignores me, climbing into her sleeping bag.

I grab my backpack and search through the pockets, cursing myself for never carrying cash. "Is there something I can do for you? Some way to thank you?" I find my metro card and hold it out. It's newly loaded. "You can have this?"

She turns her flinty gaze on me. "Fuck off. Can't a body get some sleep around here?"

I consider leaving the card where she'll find it. But she doesn't want it. She made that clear. I tuck it back in its pocket and head in the opposite direction from where Isaac ran. I don't know where I'm going. It doesn't even matter.

When I was Lady Guinevere back in middle school, I was so angry at the notion that I needed to be saved, that we kept telling this story where damsels are in distress and only saved when some brave knight appears to rescue them. I wanted the damsels to use their brains and cunning and save themselves.

And even though my rescuer today was a lady knight, it still feels hollow. I don't want to have needed a rescuer.

Except I did.

And so did Nor. But no one came for her.

Sometimes rescue is necessary. It doesn't mean the damsel's weak. It means the monster is monstrous.

Maybe we tell these stories of peril and rescue not to point out how strong and valiant the knights are, how honorable for happening upon a scene and displaying the very basic human decency of doing what they can to ease someone's suffering. Maybe it's more about how messed up it is that the damsels can't walk through the world without encountering a dragon at every turn.

Traveling alone

I

~~Nothing even happened why am I still~~
shaking

CHAPTER TWENTY

Lady Snowblood: a 1973 Japanese film about a woman conceived for no other reason than to seek gory revenge on the gang who raped her mother and killed her family. Written, directed, and produced by men.

Kill Bill: a 2003 film about a woman seeking revenge on the assassins who tried to kill her at her wedding. Despite asking for a stunt driver, the lead actor (who was sexually assaulted by the producer) was forced to do a dangerous driving scene and crashed, leaving her with a permanently damaged neck. Written, directed, and produced by men.

CHAPTER TWENTY-ONE

Maybe we go back to the root, tell the stories we refused to tell the first time around, the stories where those without power have swords and those with power are accountable, where it's not just damsels and dragons, but villagers and nuns and parents and wolves and herbwives and hedge-priests and everyone forming a society where taking what's not yours had consequences.

Maybe then I'll stop feeling his hands on me.

I TENSE UP
the instant
I sense
I'm not alone.

I TENSE UP
the instant
I sense
I'm not alone.

Distant hoofbeats draw nearer
but I've exhausted Minuit;
we cannot run. I urge him farther
into the woods, into the twisting paths
that may not lead us to a village
but I hope will be enough
to hide us from sight.

WHEN BIRDCALLS AND
wind rustling through leaves
replace the distant hoofbeats
I reward Minuit
with a rest by the stream.

I collapse on the grass nearby,
legs sore, heart pounding
desperate to will away the horrors

> Mother
> Father
> the captain of the guard
> Mother's lady's maid
> the footmen
> stable boys

all slaughtered.
Helene lives
and that is something
though is she any better off

alive?

WHEN THE HOOFBEATS
return, relentless,
there's no time to hide.

My heart thuds as I throw on
my hood, cower between
Minuit and the stream,
hope somehow these riders
will not see me
will not wonder at
the horse alone.

All my childhood
wanting to be seen
and now I cower.

But childhood's over now.

MARGUERITE?

Only by grasping
Minuit's bridle
do I keep from toppling

                into the stream.

I peek out to see
Emilde and Helene
on our tawny mare,
Zahra astride another horse.

What are you doing here?

Zahra gives me a look
that requires no words.
It's an absurd question,
coming from me.

I fling my arm
toward Zahra's mount.

You stole from the nuns?

               You didn't leave us much choice.

Mother would slap Emilde
for her insolence.

            Or rather,
            Helene didn't.

Zahra recounts
how Helene woke them

in a panic well before dawn,
showed them my empty
spot in the bed, then
headed for the stables
saddled a horse
and seemed intent
on taking off alone
in search of me.

Though she is the elder
I am not sure Helene
has ever been the one
to come to my rescue.

Not that I need rescuing.

I NEARLY SOB WITH RELIEF.
I am no longer alone

and yet

I flood with fury.

Do they have
any idea
what I intend
to do?

EMILDE HELPS HELENE
off the horse,
leads her to me,
the horse to water.

I reach out and
tug my sister down
to join me on the grass.

She leans her head
on my shoulder.
I rest my head
gently on hers.

So fragile and yet there is a core
of steel inside somewhere.

*Do you want
to go back?*

She grips my hand
and there's the steel.

No. We can never go back.

CHAPTER TWENTY-TWO

Jess's house is glass and steel and modern art and money. Lavish flower arrangements on every surface are the only indication people might actually live here.

"Did someone die?" I touch my finger to the stamen of a lily and rub the orange residue between my fingers.

"My parents' marriage." Jess leads me through the common living areas, which look as though no one has lived communally in them since the house was bought, leads me past art worth more than the car my parents share, a sculpture that could probably finance my college education.

That month we had cold showers because my parents simply couldn't afford to replace the broken water heater, I looked with longing at houses like these, all money and excess, cold showers only as part of some detox-cleanse-fitness regimen. But now that I'm inside a house like this? I wouldn't want to live here.

Jess's room is another planet. There's not an inch of wall space, between the inspiration boards for medieval costume designs, snapshots of Jess and Summer and other theater kids, show posters I recognize from the school's drama department, band posters that mean nothing to me, a large case displaying swords, and a prominent plaque for winning the district-wide spelling bee in middle school.

Jess beams at the plaque. "I won with *eudaemonic*. You should have seen the look on Marissa Solomon's face."

Even the high ceiling is covered, but it's covered with an abstract mural, all swirling eddies and black holes, northern lights, a shimmering abyss. It makes our underwater mural in Nor's room look like preschool finger painting.

"You like?" Jess says. "That took me an entire summer."

I can't even picture how they did it—it was hard enough for Nor and me to paint her regular ceiling—unless they rigged up some Sistine Chapel setup. "How did you . . . ?"

"I have my ways." They flop on the bed and a framed photo on the nightstand clatters over. I reach to set it upright but: "Leave it," they say. "Serves Summer right for abandoning me."

I have to look now. Jess and Summer are a few years younger, at the giant fountain in Seattle Center. It might be Bumbershoot or Folklife. There are a ton of people in the background, but Jess and Summer have eyes only for each other.

"She's your best friend, isn't she?"

Jess rolls their face into a pillow and mumbles something.

"You're lucky. To have a friend like that."

They sit up and take the frame from me. "Shut up. I know. I'm such a baby. I just really wish I weren't home all summer."

I try to ignore the twinge of hurt. If they'd gone to theater camp, they wouldn't have gotten to know me, wouldn't be working with me on Marguerite's story. But that's me being selfish—again. If they were away at camp, they also wouldn't have had to listen to their parents argue all summer.

"It's hard to describe," Jess says, "but this camp is the greatest place in the world."

I laugh. "Is that all?"

"It's this bubble where we're not the theater weirdos, or we are, but we're all theater weirdos, and the weirder you are, it's almost like the higher your status is, because there's still status or whatever, but it works completely differently."

"And yours is high?"

"Obviously. I mean, (a) because I'm amazing. But also because I've been going there since sixth grade, so everyone knows me and the counselors all love me and it feels more like home than home."

That wouldn't be hard, though. To feel more like home than this museum.

"Thank god you're here for the summer," they say, pulling me down onto the bed. "I'm going to do something amazing with your hair."

They reach to grab a hairbrush off the nightstand and my heart speeds up, someone bigger and stronger, arms wrapping around me from behind.

If that woman hadn't been there on the steps—

"You okay?"

But this is Jess. "Yeah. Go for it." I take a steadying breath and try to breathe away the hands gripping me tighter even as I said get off. It's so stupid, nothing compared to Nor.

I focus on the hands in my hair, soothing on my scalp. I let Jess's chatter roll over me like a lullaby, something about the last show they did at drama camp. By the time they're done, my breathing is normal and I've almost forgotten those other hands. Almost. A French braid wraps like a crown around my head.

"Whoa . . ."

Jess shrugs and jumps off the bed. "Okay, so, I had an ulterior motive for inviting you over."

I figured, since we've been hanging out for weeks, and anytime I mention going to their house, they have a reason it isn't the right time.

"My parents are splitting up their assets or whatever. Selling stuff off to pay for legal fees, they say, but mostly to piss each other off. And these"— Jess gestures toward the display case of swords like a game-show host— "are worth some serious cash."

I approach the case. It's filled with weapons I've learned about in my research. Not blunt-tipped reproductions, but the real thing. These weapons have spilled blood. Longswords and spears, a falchion, a flail.

My eye is drawn to something smaller, but still deadly looking. The blade is around a foot long, tapering into a sharp point that could puncture chain mail.

"You like the rondel dagger?" Jess opens the case and pulls it out. "Rondel because of the rounded hand guard and the pommel on the end, see?"

Jess points out the beautifully carved and rounded grip, and my hand reaches out, greedy. I have to hold it. It fits my palm perfectly, and unlike the massive swords at Mack's class that I can barely lift, this was made for me.

"Would Marguerite have used something like this?"

"Sure," Jess says, eyes bright. "They were carried into battle all the time, a standard sidearm by Marguerite's day. Richard the Third's postmortem showed a rondel wound to the head!"

I hold it out in front of me, feel it like an extension of my own body. "It wouldn't be a match for a sword, though."

Jess shrugs. "Different uses is all. By the time you're fighting with a rondel, you're too close for a sword to be practical. Also a lot easier to land a surprise blow with a smaller weapon. Works for Arya Stark."

"And your parents are selling them?" There are a lot more valuable things in this house than some old swords.

Jess takes the rondel from me and returns it to the case. "Most of them belonged to my dad's brother, Alistair. Who my mom slept with."

My eyes bug out.

"He's dead and they never come in here, so out of sight, out of mind, but I think if either one of them remembers I exist—I mean the swords exist—they would summon the auctioneer so fast someone could cut off a hand."

I tug on the end of my braid. "How can I help?"

"I'm so glad you asked!" Jess grins. "We're going to keep them at your house for a while."

"My house? But your parents—"

Jess waves a breezy hand. "Won't miss them if they don't see them. That's the point."

How could anyone have something so valuable and not miss it when it's taken away? It feels like stealing, if they're really worth so much money. Maybe it feels wrong because now that it's a possibility, I want them like I want Nor to come back home. I want a whole armory; I want a dagger at my side that's an extension of my fury.

"Sure," I say. "If it'll help."

———

Through the magic of a supremely uncurious Lyft driver, we manage to transport the weapons. Less than a mile separates our houses, but they're sets from completely different films.

The gleam of wealth so bright it hurts the eyes, but no amount of priceless art can save the marriage. Major studio production, total Oscar bait.

The ramshackle home so cozy it attracts all strays, but the family at its center cannot hold themselves together. Quirky indie starring that one guy from the show you used to love.

Mom talks about the Seattle of her teens, when Fremont was filled with blue-collar dockworkers, when the fishmongers at Pike Place Market could actually afford to live in the city where they entertained tourists, when Nirvana was nirvana and even kids in thrift-store flannel could afford a concert ticket.

But things change, except for all the things that never do.

I have to haul some stuff out from under my bed, but once it's clear, the whole case fits neatly underneath. A bit unceremonious for valuable antiques, but we're keeping them safe. And even if Mom or Papi happen upon them, Jess insists my parents love them and their eccentricities so explaining why I'm storing their weapons should be no problem.

Mom comes home bubbling over with excitement because a short story she wrote got accepted to an obscure literary journal. She's been sending stuff out for years, stacking up piles of rejections, almost never getting any feedback, much less published. It always seemed so pointless to me. Why keep writing if no one's ever going to read it?

For the first time, I kind of get it.

I'm writing Marguerite's story for me. I thought that's how it would stay. I wasn't trying to write the Great American Novel or whatever. (That's for white dudes anyway, right?) But now Jess is involved, invested. Which I love, but it adds this whole other layer. What if no one had ever read it? If a girl tells a story but there's no one there to hear it, did it even happen?

Papi comes home with flowers and sparkling cider, which he drops on the kitchen counter so he can grab Mom by the waist and twirl her around. I hope he doesn't throw his back out.

Jess watches it all unfold, bemused. Then they begin bustling about the kitchen like some sort of servant, pulling out wineglasses with a flourish, draping a dish towel over their forearm. It's an act, a way to cover the hurt, I think, of watching a happy marriage.

Or maybe Jess is genuinely happy, folded into a family where no one's screaming or selling off contentious heirlooms.

Jess serves the cider and fills a glass for me, but I leave it on the counter. It's sickly sweet and reminds me of the day we found out Nor had been accepted into the University of Washington.

Of course she was accepted into the University of Washington. She was a top student, on one of the best high school newspapers in the country, internship at the aquarium, volunteer at the library, even a couple years on the track team.

But when we found out, we celebrated like she'd gotten into Harvard. Mom and Papi both cried, there was bubbly (or our version anyway, since my parents both come from hearty lines of alcoholics and never touch a drop), and then we all piled into the car and headed to one of those shops full of overpriced stuff branded with the university's mascot and colors.

Purple reign! Go dawgs!

We left with sweatshirts and pennants, ball caps, and even a stuffed Husky. For the next week, gas and groceries went on a credit card, but we did it anyway. This was the dream, land of opportunity, only up from here.

———

When the house is quiet, I pull out the weapons and lay them on my bed.

There are three longswords, and one is significantly larger than the others. I run my hand along the blade. It's smooth and flawless, like Jess has been polishing it, readying themselves for the battle to come.

The hilt is filigreed like the one Jess first drew in the margins of my notebook. I realize with a start that the sword is one and the same. When I try to lift it, it's nothing like the prop swords we used in the church basement. I can barely hold it one-handed. Doing battle would be unthinkable.

But even the act of holding it sends a surge of power through me. Marguerite's longing for a sword as she forges her path through the world makes perfect sense. The idea that a girl, stripped of everything but her grief and rage, might see no other options? It's more real than ever before. If I'd been holding this weapon instead of an umbrella—

A weapon would have done nothing for Nor, though. By the time she got dragged behind the frat house, it was too late for that. By the time she was born, it was too late for that. Our world had already decided that a boy like Craig could take what he wanted from a girl like Nor.

So defense, prevention, justice are impossible.

Which leaves only revenge.

PERSONAL FRIENDS

HE CHATEAU AT ANJOU
sprawls along the Loire River
much grander than my memories.

Shouldn't it be the reverse:

> those childhood moments
> reflected against the wall of memory
> absurdly large, blurred edges.

Like the jump off the dock
into shallow water
so monumental to a child,
epic leap off a cliff
onto jagged rocks below
survived only because
I was so brave.

The water
is no longer
shallow
and I don't know
how to swim.

I lead Minuit;
Emilde leads
the convent's horse
                    (heaven forgive us)
to the gate
that keeps the peasants
from their betters.

I've no idea which we are.
The answer comes quickly.

> *No beggars.*

I watch the guard's hand.
It does not go to his sword
as it would for a greater threat
than four bedraggled girls.

> *Begging your pardon,*
> Emilde begins.

I am no beggar.
I employ my haughtiest voice.
*I am the daughter of
Monsieur Georges de Bressieux
and a personal friend
to the Duchess Isabella of Lorraine.*

He grunts.
> *I'll be your personal
> friend, chérie.*

My hands grasp
for the sword I do not have.

200

I would slit his throat so fast
his blood would drench
these convent clothes,
the grass, the gate, my rage.

Emilde's voice surprises,
friendly, warm.

>   *You hail from Brioude*
>   *if I am not mistaken, friend?*

I glance at her
but she avoids my eyes.

>   *I recognize your rhythms.*
>   *Hard to forget, even after*
>   *years in service.*

A hint of camaraderie,
demeanor changing.

>   *Grew up along the Allier.*
>   *I've just returned*
>   *from burying my pa.*

Emilde makes
the sign of the cross
and he grunts again.

>   *The world is better off,*
>   *believe you me.*

Emilde laughs;
I've never heard her
laugh before.

Do you know
Old Melisende,
by chance?

The herbwife?
She only delivered me
into this world!

We are saved by the herbwife,
Emilde's grand-mère—
or so she claims.

We're sent to the servants' entrance,
granted admission to the kitchens
and welcomed for a spell to rest and eat
though still no one believes my station.

The guard's hands wander
as he ushers us into the kitchen.

Let me know
if you need help
getting warm.

202

EMILDE AND ZAHRA SPEAK
the language of servants,
seat us at their table,
procure bread and butter, tea.

The household help
eye us, invaders.
They hardly know
invaders, though.

I watch for one who might believe me,
relay a message to the duchess.
I'm rallying the courage to ask
the last one in the kitchen
as the candles are extinguished.

Then she speaks.

> *When you've had your fill*
> *you'll bed down in the stables.*
> *Be gone by dawn, you hear?*
> *This ain't no home for strays.*

I push to my feet
ready to breathe fire
on this insubordinate.

Helene grabs my arm,
pulls me down, tucks her chin.
She speaks, for only
the second time, since . . .

> *Yes, madame.*
> *Thank you, madame.*

Emilde shakes her head
as the woman grunts, retreats.
I think her scorn is for the woman.
Instead she turns on me.

> *We only just got in.*
> *You'd see us thrown out*
> *as night falls?*

I whirl on the kitchen girl
who oversteps again and again.

That wretch may not know
I am her superior
but you ought to.

A bell jangles
before she can retort.
Our heads all whip
to the wall of bells,
each attached to a tiny sign
carved with a different name.

I'm still puzzling them out
when the wretch returns.

> *Bloody hell,*
> *which one was it?*

Zahra is quick to answer.

> *Far right.*

The woman frowns.

> *You're sure?*

> *Yes, madame.*

As soon as she's gone
Zahra grabs my arm.

> *The duchess rang*
> *for her lady's maid.*

I do not see
how that helps us.

> *I sent that woman elsewhere.*
> *You must go to the duchess!*

I run.

CHAPTER TWENTY-THREE

I write.

My parents carry on, grading papers and fixing leaks.

I write.

Jess doodles in my margins, regales me with tales of summer camps long past, disappears when their aunt whisks them away from the family drama for a few days in Victoria.

I write.

Nor does whatever Nor does now. We bring a meal over to her apartment one Sunday afternoon and my parents take it in with careful looks devoid of judgment. Her roommates add me on social media.

I write.

Instead of sleeping, I write. Instead of eating, I write. Instead of letting my brain stop long enough to remember Isaac's hands confining me, his entitlement to my body, how much worse it could have been if even one detail of the story got changed—we were inside, I was intoxicated, that woman hadn't been driven by trauma or addiction or Seattle's wild inequity to camp on the church steps with a blade in her hand—I write.

BUTTERFLY

RACE THROUGH CORRIDORS,
head down, feeling by instinct
for Isabella's chambers.

Even with the cap and apron
Zahra hurled at me as I raced
from the kitchen, it was folly
to think I could ascend unnoticed
to the upper levels and stumble
upon the proper chambers.

I've reached the main floor
and up yet one more staircase
before my heart sinks
all the way back down
to the cellars.

You, girl.

A male voice
pins me where I stand,
a butterfly trapped.

Panic rises.

*You're the new
chambermaid?*

I fight for breath.
There's still a chance.

*What on God's
green earth
are you wearing?*

I'm . . . I'm sorry, sir.

*Go back downstairs,
be fitted for your uniform
before you venture up again.*

I curtsy,
turn to go.

Wait.

Merde.

*You are not
a chambermaid.*

I take a half step back,
debate how far I'd get
if I should run—

De Bressieux?

I won't
be running
anywhere.

COOL CLOTH ON MY FOREHEAD
murmured voices at my side
sweet smell that belies
the sweat and horse and grime
caked into my skin.

She wakes, René!

A woman.

Marguerite, my dear?

I turn to see this one
who knows my name,
remembering only then
the man had known
my name as well.

A face, apple-cheeked,
older than mine but
younger than Mother's
and so much warmer.

Duchess?

She laughs.

Isabella, please!
You've broken into my home.
I think we can speak as friends.

My eyes follow the man's
warm chuckle, find him
leaning against the fireplace.
The man from the hallway.

You remember René?

René. Such a simple name
for the Duke of Lorraine,
King of Naples, husband
of the woman who might
be my salvation.

That is, if he does not
decide to th

CHAPTER TWENTY-FOUR

I fumble for my phone as it buzzes in the dark.

I'm already awake. I'm awake because there's no sleeping when Marguerite is this close to the weapons she needs. But it's the dead quiet time of night when phones should not be ringing and I cannot stop the immediate surge of heart into throat.

Oh god, Em, there's a used condom right next to me . . .

But it's Jess, not Nor. They're crying, but different from how Nor cried that night, on that call.

It's finally happened. Their dad is moving to San Francisco. Their mom is fleeing to Saipan for the rest of the summer while strangers pack up the art and antiquities and sell the house. Jess has to go with one of them.

Annoyance surges through me and I wrap my hand around the rondel dagger that has taken up residence underneath my pillow. I breathe. Poor baby. A luxury high-rise in a city of diversity and culture, or a tropical island paradise. Since I've met them, they've talked constantly about wishing their parents would get it over with. Now it's happening. Dreams come true.

"Can I come over?" they say.

But Marguerite has only just come face-to-face with Isabella. "You're going to be fine," I say. "I'll call you in the morning."

APOLOGY

YOU NEED TO REST.

Isabella turns the cloth
on my forehead.
The sky outside
is pitch-black.

René knew me by Father's ring
but Isabella didn't need
a crest to know I was the girl
who'd stabbed at hay bales
with fury but no skill.

Now I have both.

My sister—

> *Helene is safe in chambers*
> *with her lady's maid.*
> *Your maid awaits you*
> *in the adjoining room.*

I take all this in
struggle to form words
to explain our presence
but there's no need.

> *Sleep now.*
> *You've had a journey.*
> *And I suspect*
> *you've traveled*
> *more than miles.*

I DO NOT WAKE AGAIN
until the sun is high
and Zahra bustles about
fresh and clean
and newly uniformed.

It's any other morning.
                              But it's not.

Helene?

            She's found the library.

Did she sleep?

Zahra pauses.

            I heard her scream.
            But when I checked
            Emilde's lullabies
            had done the trick.

I sit up.
Emilde can soothe my sister
in the night, but I will destroy
the ones who made her scream.

I DON THE GARMENTS ZAHRA LAYS OUT,
though they're far too fine.
I will not be taken seriously
running through the halls
in traveling rags.

I do not, however, wash.
I've more important things
to consider than grime
beneath my nails.

Besides
the worst of it
will never
be washed
away.

THE FIRST SERVANT DOES NOT UNDERSTAND
my questions. A simpleton, I think,
or else they don't speak French.

I don't consider that perhaps
my words are all ajumble,
like my mind, my heart.

I interrupt the next
on hands and knees,
scrubbing the stones of the great hall.
She sighs, but has the answer I seek:

> *The duchess has gone out*
> *for her morning ride.*

THE ESTATE IS
grander than Father's,
but stables are stables.

The familiar smell,
the light creeping in
through cracks in the walls,
the graceful beasts.

I sink onto a pile of hay
let myself set down
the unwieldy shield
I've been carrying for days
and give myself a moment
in which I do not fear
for my sister's safety,
Zahra's, Emilde's,
the other women.

With only animal eyes upon me,
no expectations, pressing decisions,
nothing but the crushing weight
of living in this world, I am

only Marguerite.

But perhaps that is
most terrifying of all.

WHICH IS WORSE:

to imagine
I could have
done something
and didn't

or

to face
the crushing truth
I never
had a chance.

A STABLE BOY'S APPEARANCE
reminds me I am never

only Marguerite.

Even in this refuge
there are men, intruders.

He is small, pimply,
laughable to think
he might be a threat
and yet
sometimes
those are the ones
most worthy of fear.

*Can I help you,
mademoiselle?*

To stand, display
my finery and obvious rank,
or maintain my position,
Father's move of power
to intimidate inferiors.

Mademoiselle?

I stumble to my feet displaying
not so much rank and finery
as exhaustion, nerves.

*I am a guest of the duchess.
I await her return.*

Surely mademoiselle
would be more comfortable—

I am a guest of the duchess.
I await her return.

This one speaks perfect French
and I am through with men
who act as though
they cannot comprehend
simple words
because they've fallen
from the mouth of a woman.

THE STABLE BOY GONE,
I stay on my feet,
catch my balance
so I do not look the fool
when Isabella returns.

How can I expect
her help, her confidence,
if I can barely take two steps

without stumbling
on the bodies in my wake?

IT SEEMS YOU ARE
a personal friend
of the duchess, after all.

I whirl around
at the sound of a voice
not the spindly stable boy's.

The guard
from the night before.

You clean up
real nice.

My heart thuds.
I grasp for a sword
I'll never hold again.

My stumble backward
is my first mistake;
I end up cornered.

I owe you
an apology.

He steps toward me,
slow, like he's no threat
except we both know
he's nothing but.

If it weren't for
your pretty little friend—

Emilde—

—I'd have turned you
noble ladies out
in the night.
But ladies like you
deserve to be kept
warm and safe,
secure behind walls.

He's an arm's length away.
I could stab him if only—

I glance wildly around.
The tools on the wall
are promising, but
he's too close
for pitchfork, whip—

What's wrong, chérie?
Nothing to fear.
You're safe now.

He reaches out a hand,
trails a finger down
the side of my face.
I meet his gaze,
let him drink in
the fear in my eyes,
his intoxicant of choice

distracting while
my hand lashes out
grabs the hoof pick
from the wall—
its short, curved blade

the perfect size
to thrust against his neck
force him against the stall
draw a bead of blood
while he struggles
the terror reversed.

HOOFBEATS APPROACH
but I do not move.
I'll not give up this prey.

Your form has improved.

Your Grace!

He cries out desperately
to the duchess, pleads
with a woman to save him.

This madwoman—

*I think
she's not so mad.
Provoked, perhaps?*

Isabella takes her time
removing her horse's saddle,
leading him to his stall.

I keep my gaze
pinned on my prey,
blade to his neck
enjoying his fear.

How many throats
pulsing, alive
do I need to feel
on the tip of my blade
before I'm safe?

I falter.

The moment I do
he spins away
from my weapon
and straight into
the tip of another blade.

Isabella holds
her dagger casually

> a lace fan
> a parasol
> a deadly weapon.

> *His crime, then?*

> *No crime—*

> *I'm not asking you.*

Her gaze flits
from him to me
then back to him.
She won't falter.

But what was his crime?
I know how he made me feel
last night at the gate, in the kitchen,
and now, with his hand on my face

but a man will hardly
find himself convicted
of touching a maiden
on the face.

> *I only meant
> to serve her needs—*

With a flick
of her wrist,
the noble lady

Queen of Naples
Duchess of Lorraine
slices the fabric of his tunic
and also, judging by his howl,
his flesh as well.

Rope.

She juts her chin toward the wall
where I found the hook.

I grab a length of rope.

You do the honors.

CHAPTER TWENTY-FIVE

Jess's phone goes straight to voicemail when I call in the morning. Which might not be morning so much as late afternoon, because I slept until nearly noon and then wrote for hours. But they'll understand. They understand passions more than anyone else I know.

Except Nor, maybe.

I'm sure that in the light of day, they're feeling better.

When they don't answer or respond to texts by dark, I assume they're huffy I didn't tell them to come straight over in the middle of the night. Maybe I'm a terrible friend.

But really? They've been pretty clear I'm a second-choice friend anyway. I'm wrestling with a lot and they know it. Their big crisis was that the thing they knew was going to happen actually happened. I don't blame them for being upset, but this was one disaster they should have seen coming.

I do the only thing left: I write.

WE

I'LL NEED A REASON
to detain him.

Isabella plucks hay
from the waist of my gown
as the dungeon's heavy doors
clang shut behind us.

He has a wife,
children.

If he's released
we won't be safe here.
I'll need a new plan.

Isabella takes my arm
before I can escape
up the stairs.

I believe you.
Whatever happened,
I believe you.

It wasn't—
Nothing happened.

She nods.

But it was going to?

If you hadn't arrived—

That's all I need.
He won't trouble you again.

Her warm fingers
slide down my arm
until they slip into my hand

      small, cold

hold me tight
guide me up
into the light.

YOU'LL NEED WEAPONS.
Training, preparation.

Isabella's hound
follows her pace for pace
across the sitting room.

I've been trained.

For battle?

I hesitate.

You flinch like that in the field
and you'll be impaled
on the end of Chalon's sword.

Father taught me
rules and decorum,
no different really
than Mother's table manners.

But what was the use
of empty techniques
when battle is kill
            or be killed?
I may as well have
learned embroidery.
At least then when
I stabbed my target
there'd be an end result.

YOUR SWORD WORK
hand-to-hand
is excellent.
I worry, though,
how you will fare
atop a moving horse.

I could slip out
in the night,
make my way
to the camp
of the Prince of Orange

A mace and battle ax
are useful at close range
as they can smash a helmet
and kill a man on contact.

run my sword
through him
and die
by his men
whose rage would burn
hotter when their general
dies at the hands of a girl.

I do not care to battle
with a lance, for once
your opponent is impaled
he's dead, but you're
without a weapon. Still,
we must bring lances
or we won't—

Wait, we?

She stops pacing.
Her hound stops too.

> *Of course we.*
> *Did you think*
> *I'd let you*
> *go alone?*

CHAPTER TWENTY-SIX

I'm not a total asshole. When a few more days go by without a response from Jess, I track down a number for Summer and text her. Jess said Camp Theater Paradise didn't have good cell service, but surely teens marooned on an island for an entire summer find a way.

Summer responds within a day. Jess left town.

That's my first clue that I was a bigger jerk than I'd realized. I scour their social media, find few updates. Finally, a photo of Jess with a severely beautiful woman on a boat. All the time they've spent with my family this summer and I've never seen their mother once.

So they went to Saipan. They had to be seriously pissed off to go all the way across the globe to escape me.

But there I go being self-centered again. Probably the decision had nothing to do with me. Maybe.

PENNYROYAL TEA

Of course
I thought
I was alone.

Parents dead
brother gone

sister walled in
like an anchoress

        Zahra a friend
        but set apart
        by station

I have only
myself
and my sword.

And still
I do not
have a sword.

Helene insists
on taking midday meal
in the kitchen.

Isabella flutters a hand.

Wherever she's comfortable.

I seat myself
with the duchess
and her husband,
who only ever gazes
upon her with adoration.

*I am so sorry
for all you've been through.*

Does he know?
Does he have any idea
what we've been through?

It's so vague

what we've been through

a rainstorm
a touch of fever
the brutal slaughter
of our entire household

but his eyes are kind, sincere.
Isabella places a hand
over his on the table,
rests there, as though
touching a man
does not have to be
the most repulsive thing.

MARINATED LEEKS
in mustard vinaigrette
aromatic sausages
with cinnamon and cloves
fava bean soup
freshly baked bread and
spiced quince butter cake

are spread before us
on the table

and though I have not
had a proper meal
in days, my stomach turns.

Perhaps Helene
has the right idea—
bread and pottage
with the servants
feels more fitting

and yet
I'll need my strength
for the road ahead.

I reach for
a helping of leeks
and the duchess
is the one who bolts
from the table
retching.

SHALL I RING
for her lady's maid?

> *I'll go.*
> *Pardon me.*

René dashes
from the room.
I am left alone
save a servant in the corner
to eat the vegetables
before me.

I do not even care
for leeks.

ISABELLA FINDS ME
in the courtyard
dueling air.

>*Let's get you*
>*a real weapon.*

She strides past me
across the bailey,
hound on her heels.
I stumble to catch up.

Are you well? We don't have to—

>*I cannot abide fava beans.*
>*The armory will have*
>*what you need.*

Father's estate did not have
a proper armory, only
a room in the east wing
devoted to his weapons.

Isabella's armory
is a cavernous chamber
opposite the stables
filled to bursting
with swords and daggers
polearms, maces, flails
longbows, halberds, shields

>and armor that might
>even fit my frame.

ORNATE FILIGREE
on the cross guard
of a beautiful sword
draws my attention.

> *Stunning, isn't it?*

Isabella hands me
a simpler weapon.

> *But this is easier to maneuver*
> *and a far sharper blade.*

I take the sword,
test its weight, possibility.

> *The weapon*
> *is not as important*
> *as your skill.*
> *But the weapon*
> *is still*
> *important.*

She takes her own
simple sword.

> *Let's see how much*
> *your technique has improved*
> *since you were a child.*

THREE TIMES I'VE
disarmed the duchess
when Zahra appears,
out of breath.

> *Begging your pardon, miss,*
> *but your sister is unwell.*

Swords clatter to the ground
as we hurry to the kitchen,
the enormous dog
storming the threshold before us.

> *Get that mangy beast*
> *out of my kitchen!*

The same miserable woman
who would have sent us to the barn
shakes a cleaver at the hound
before going cloud white at the sight
of his mistress on his heels.

> *That mangy beast*
> *has a name, which is Owen,*
> *and he will go*
> *where he pleases*
> *in my home.*

The maid sinks
into a curtsy so low I fear
she may not rise again.

> *Yes, madame.*
> *Begging pardon, madame.*

Zahra beckons us
to a far corner.

She's here.

Searching for Helene
in a kitchen, among servants—

my mind stutters
on the horrors
of that night

—which is why
Isabella gets there first
crouches down
her servants looking on
curious but not surprised
and reaches a hand
into a cabinet.

Helene, love?

MY SISTER WEDGED HERSELF
inside a dumbwaiter
while I was playing knight.

> *I went to send*
> *tea up to the library*
> *and there she was!*

A distressed kitchen girl
mangles her apron
between white-knuckled fists.

Where is Emilde? Her lady's maid?

The tetchy one grunts.

> *Put her to work. She's help, ain't she?*
> *Houseguests mean extra labors.*
> *Their servants don't sit around.*

She withers slightly
under Isabella's gaze.

> *Ain't she help?*

Helene shrieks
when Isabella touches her,
tries to shrink farther back.

Let me.

But before I can reach my sister,
Owen is there, wet nose prodding,
reaching something I never will.

Coaxed out by Isabella's dog,
Helene refuses any touch
except his prodding snout.

Emilde is beside herself
when she returns to find
her lady disturbed.

> *She only wanted*
> *to feel safe!*
> *Is that so hard?*

I very nearly reprimand her
but Isabella's grip
on my arm reminds me

Emilde has watched over
my sister more keenly
than I ever have.

> *We're so sorry.*

The duchess speaks to Emilde
as though this lowly servant
were equal to the queen of Naples.

> *I'm sure we can find*
> *a way for Helene*
> *to feel safe away*
> *from prying eyes?*

> *She feels safest*
> *in a kitchen . . .*

Emilde trails off.
She can't explain it
any more than Helene can,
Helene, who sits, mute,
arms around Owen
as though he were the only one
tethering her to this world.

ISABELLA SENDS FOR THE PHYSICIAN
who prescribes herbs and teas
and tinctures to soothe and calm,
the tiniest plug in the dam
holding back an ocean of pain.

After hushed conversation
with the duchess, the physician
inquires if any of my party
require further care.
Pennyroyal tea
and pomegranates
juniper and rue
catnip, sage, cypress, tansy
hellebore, hyssop, dittany, and opium

      so many options
      it's almost as though
      he's seen this before.

THAT BLUR OF TERROR
in my bedchamber
was not creation
of a life. It was
          destruction

except

it is not always
one or else the other.
The two go
sword in scabbard
          sometimes.

To carry a child is a risk
when done for love or obligation
but to carry a seed that's taken root
after invaders pillaged a land
for their

CHAPTER TWENTY-SEVEN

Papi's knock scatters the words.

"I don't want any lasagna," I call.

"My hands are full, can you open the door?"

I sigh from the middle of my bed, where I'm surrounded by Marguerite and various research books open to specific pages around me. Sometimes the history falls together in absurdly perfect puzzle pieces—René's brother-in-law being the newly crowned king of France, for example. Maybe he can get word to the generals Marguerite will need—

"Canchita?"

I climb off my bed, trying to cause minimal disturbance. Not wanting lasagna doesn't mean I want room service that will only make me feel guilty for not sitting in the kitchen with him while my mom's out at her monthly girls' night.

Instead, I find Papi holding a stack of shoeboxes. I hold the door open and he brings them in, Chester nosing in after him, leaping up onto my bed, and knocking multiple books off.

"Chester, no!"

"Nor told me you guys are working on a project para tu mamá," Papi says. "I dug these out. Thought they might help."

I haven't thought about the scrapbook since I went searching for photos in the basement and instead found my mom's dissertation on female vengeance films, which was obviously more interesting. Now Papi's done the work of digging out photos for me and I repay him with annoyance.

His eyes fall on the Moleskine. "It's good to see that again," he says as I try to save my books from Chester galumphing around on my bed for the perfect spot. "You said you lost it."

"It turned up."

He sits on the end of my bed. "The school told me, ¿sabías? The middle school? When that little cerote stole your notebook and spread your private words around."

I sit on the other end of the bed, closing my hand over the edge of the rondel dagger and pushing it farther under my pillow. "You never said anything."

"I figured your privacy had been invaded enough. You'd tell me if you wanted to."

"It was embarrassing."

"That boy was an embarrassment. Hijuela . . . Expressing your feelings isn't wrong."

"I know."

He hesitates and I think our little heart-to-heart is over, but he goes on. "Tu mamá and I are so thrilled you're writing. You've got such a gift. Pero me preocupa que you're skipping meals—"

"I'm not hungry, Papi. I'll eat later, I promise. Thanks for the photos."

"Claro. It's nice of you girls to do something. I'd hoped for her birthday we could have a getaway . . . ¿Victoria o algo? But it doesn't look like that's going to happen."

Papi hasn't been getting as many plumbing disaster calls lately. I've overheard hushed conversations with Mom about whether she can manage to take on some extra online classes. (She can't.) Sometimes she suggests he look for teaching jobs—he has an MFA in poetry, after all. But when his work is steady, he actually makes more as a plumber than he would as an adjunct professor.

Which seems messed up, but the world needs pipes to reliably carry away our shit more than it needs poetry.

It's cynical of me, but I can't keep from wondering whether Husky fans spread word to harm Papi's business. Maybe after my hashtag debacle. Add financial stress to the list of things that are my fault.

As Papi slips out the door, I reach under my pillow and wrap my hand around the dagger.

ENTITLED

Isabella puts me through my paces
morning, noon and in the night
we fill the gaps that Father left:

        strategy
        geography
        patriarchy.

I knew our world
was ruled by men—
I've grown up sheltered,
not blindfolded, gagged
and cut off from all discourse.

But I've had the luxury
of ignorance to how men think,
how men are raised to feel
themselves entitled to the world.

I thought it a quirk of my brother's
like my sister's love of books
and dark, quiet places.

René is my tutor
on the ways and thoughts of men,
a dedicated teacher
until the point each day
when his beloved
turns an unmistakable
shade of green.

Half a dozen children
she's carried
            René confides
even borne some
into the world
but none have lived
to celebrate a single year.

She pretends the seed
has not been planted,
doesn't grow, for if she denies
it's there, perhaps it will never die.

It's twisted logic but
sometimes
that's the only kind.

ISABELLA INSISTS ON PLANNING
as though together
we will join de Gaucourt
and the king's army,
take on Chalon and his men
past the point when it is clear
she carries a child who may yet live,
made of love and long awaited.
The only battle she will see
is childbirth.

René offers to go in her stead
but aside from the terror
on Isabella's face
at the thought of his certain death

I will have no man
by my side
when I face
Chalon.

HELENE EMERGES
slightly each day,
still silent, but
some spark of life
so long as Owen is near.

She finds a bit of fabric,
thread, and spends the days
secluded in some nook.
On sunny days, the garden,
stabbing cloth repeatedly.

I feign ignorance
that Emilde sleeps
in Helene's chambers.

She grates on me
but the kitchen girl
would fight at my side
with equal fury except
that she would never
leave my sister.

ZAHRA, THOUGH, INSISTS
she is my handmaiden
to the end, and so
she joins my lessons.

How can I ask Zahra
to join me as we hurtle
toward certain death?

And yet the blaze in her eyes
when she swings a sword
assures me I am not asking.

NEXT TO HELENE
on a wrought-iron bench
the metal upon my back
is cool like armor.

I'll be leaving soon.

She continues stabbing
at her cloth in a hoop.

You'll be safe here.

Her shoulders tense.

*The duke and duchess,
their men, this fortress . . .*

I was very nearly attacked
inside these walls.

*You'll have Emilde.
And Owen.*

The beast lifts his head,
snorts, then lays it back
on his mistress's feet.
Helene lets out a breath,
her shoulders relax.

A sudden flash of
Mother at the harp
delicate fingers flying
lost in music, the weight
of noble expectations lifted
for as long as the song would last.

I reach into the pouch at my waist
fingers saying a last goodbye
to my only connection
with the woman who bore me.

I hold out Mother's brooch.
Helene's own flying fingers
                              still.
She lets me fasten it to
the bodice of her dress
and does not flinch
at my touch.

Helene may have the brooch
but I will keep the ring
upon my finger, the one
that proclaims exactly who I am
to anyone who cares to look.

I MAY NOT RETURN.
But if I don't, Helene,
I'll have taken our revenge—
yours and mine.
I must do this.

She pauses only long enough
to raise her head,
meet my eye, and nod.

Then she renews
her diligent pursuit,
each stitch
a suture
bound to fail
the wound too great
but healing will come
not from needle and thread
but from the girl who wields them.

FOR ALL I TELL HELENE
of safety within these walls
my nights are awkward dances
with reluctant partners,
a step or two of grace
then stumble, lose the beat,
constant awareness
of every limb and breath
a desperation for dawn
the end of the song
the moment I free myself
from my suitor, the graceless night.

This night the dance
                    is interrupted
with percussive beats
that do not match the rhythm.

Hoofbeats, shouts
drawbridge lowering.

I grab the sword beside my bed.
This is the dance, the suitor I know.

CHAPTER TWENTY-EIGHT

I write and write and write but also sometimes I can't anymore.

When I reach that point (and Jess still isn't responding, which: Maybe they don't even have cell service in Saipan?), my gaze falls on the shoeboxes still sitting where Papi left them on my desk.

Nor has sent a few irritated texts wondering when I'm going to get the photos to her, since she's in charge of scrapbook layout. Sucks when your sister doesn't respond to your messages, I guess.

I pull a dusty lid off the first box and settle on the floor, since my bed and desk are full of Marguerite. These pictures go way back—Mom as a toddler, in the house she still lives in. Mom around four years old, in an astonishingly poufy dress and hat, clutching a stuffed bunny, while her brothers wrestle over an Easter basket. Mom on skates, Mom eating birthday cake, Mom winning some sort of academic award.

I pull out a few photos from each age range. They're thick and glossy, from the time before photos on phones, or even digital cameras, I think. My grandparents had to care enough to have film developed, then hold on to the tangible objects over the years, surviving the purges of stuff from my grandparents' house to college to grad school to newlywed apartment and on and on. Stuffed in a shoebox somewhere I couldn't even find them, but still.

The second shoebox has more photos, from high school, I think. Girls in overalls and flannel with arms slung around each other. Photos that follow the extended arm of the subject from hand holding the old-school camera backward toward their face—prehistoric selfies. Cheesy school-dance photos, Mom in a shiny coral dress with a pimply boy encircling her waist from behind, and another in a black strapless mini-dress with a group of girlfriends, all striking *Charlie's Angels* poses.

Mixed in with the high school photos are some report cards and essays with red As scrawled across the top. One essay has a B-, and the teacher's note says, "Beautifully written, but not the assignment. Follow the rubric next time, Kath."

Beneath that, in a loopier version of the handwriting I recognize, my mom has written, "NO ONE MADE AUSTEN WRITE TO A RU-BRIC, MISS FOSKET!!!"

I pull that out for the scrapbook, for sure.

I'm about to move on to the third shoebox when a folded piece of paper at the bottom catches my eye. I tug it from a corner where it's caught and when it comes free, I unfold it to find an unfamiliar handwriting at the bottom—it's signed Marla, which isn't a name I recognize.

The handwriting is urgent, and the first words are "PLEASE READ THIS, K." I'm expecting a glimpse into my mom's high school drama—dates for a dance, gossip gone awry, accusations of lying or cheating or stealing. But as I read on, my stomach churns.

I know you just want this to be over, but you HAVE to tell someone. Think about the other girls he's hurt. The other girls he'll hurt after we graduate. When I took you to the clinic, you promised you'd tell. Please, K.

K is Kath. My mom.

EQUAL

My brother, Philippe.
Not Chalon and his men.
My brother, my blood
has completed the task
I thought I'd have to
and now he's found us,
            his sisters.

I race to the stable,
embrace him.

            Helene is alive?
            Where is she?

These are his first words.

Asleep.
It's the middle—

            Why didn't you tell me?
            Why didn't you send word?

How was I to know
where you were?

He shakes me off, shoves
past me, heads toward
the castle, his back
a familiar sight.

What happened?
Did you find Chalon's men?

He grunts.

> *They're camped*
> *near Autun for now.*

And?

He stops,
spins on his heel.

> *And?*

Did you avenge
our honor?

He sneers.

> *What would you have me do,*
> *little sister? Get myself killed?*
> *How then would you two survive?*

He sent me
to shepherd
shattered women
when I was barely more
than shards of glass myself

into a world content
to dash our shards
our jagged selves
along the unforgiving rocks

so he could play
at furious elder brother
while doing nothing
and now, enraged, inadequate

he strikes the vessel
I've managed to rebuild
despite the cracks
the missing pieces.

How then will we survive,
my sister and I?
By our own strength.

HELENE LETS PHILIPPE SIT
at her side, resting her hand
on his, granting affection
she never grants me.

Sometimes I catch a glimpse
of the boy who didn't yet know
his status, who still believed
his sisters equal to his strength
and temper, wit, before the world
taught him such equality
would make him weak.

Sometimes I see it
and the fury rises
that he didn't care enough
to fight against the lies.

My own brother.

CHAPTER TWENTY-NINE

My own mother.

She didn't tell me. Lies or protection? It doesn't really matter which. But what if I had known this part of her story?

USELESS

EMILDE GLARES DAGGERS
at Philippe when she thinks
nobody sees, but when I catch her
I give the faintest smile, nod.

Philippe can play defender.
She and I will protect Helene.

PHILIPPE BARRICADES HIMSELF
in the library with René,
waxing bombastic about
the prince of Orange.

   Leave them to it.

Isabella drags me
away from the doors
that close in my face.

   Let him think
   his talk important.
   Your brother's arrival
   changes nothing.
   We still need to refine
   your footwork.

OUR BAGS ARE PACKED,
the horses ready.
At dinner, René lets slip
a hint of our plans
though he is meant
to keep them from Philippe.

Philippe laughs as though
it is absurd, as though
with a wife like Isabella
René would joke
about a woman's power.

My brother has always
been a fool.

AFTER DINNER ISABELLA WALKS ME
through the grounds, this refuge
where we've grown and healed,
tissue reforming, stronger than before,
prepared for the next battle.

Are you ready?

I wish she wouldn't ask.
If I consider it
I might change my mind.

You do not
have to go.

I shake her off,
walk more quickly.

Philippe thinks
the very idea
is a joke.

Your brother should know better
with you for a sister, but
he would have to care enough
to look past what the world
has told him of women.

Do you excuse him?

Of course not.

We walk in silence.

I wish
I could know
your baby.

> *My baby will know you*
> *come what may.*
> *My baby will need*
> *stories of warrior women*
> *who fight for justice*
> *with word or sword*
> *and yours will be*
> *the first she learns.*

YOU CANNOT BE SERIOUS!

Philippe throws open the doors
to my chambers, sending my heart
through the vaulted ceiling.
A man barging into a room
will never be mere annoyance again.

> *I'm so sorry!*

Zahra bursts after him.

> *He found our bags—*

> *What is this lunacy?*

Philippe's rage
almost convinces me
he cares for me,
that this isn't about
his own inability
to protect this family.

> *Charging off*
> *to be a hero?*

He sneers.

> *With your chambermaid?*
> *You can barely hold a sword!*

I can do more with a sword
than you have, else you would have
spilled some blood, rather than
slunk back to torment me!

Philippe strikes me.
Father never did
and Mother only
when I was small.

Zahra gasps
stumbles forward
and Philippe smacks her
so hard she falls to the floor.

No hesitation
I take him out at the knees
as Isabella's done to me
so many times, but far less
gently. I'm on his chest,
knee on his throat.

Tell me again
how useless I am.

CHAPTER THIRTY

Mom sits at the kitchen table, surrounded by papers, as per usual. Her coffee mug is empty.

I start pulling out the things I need to make masala chai the way Nor taught me—peppercorns, cardamom pods, cinnamon, fresh ginger, sugar, mortar and pestle. "Want some chai?"

She glances up, "Sure, sweetie. Thanks."

I put the spices into the mortar.

Mom taught us about consent in elementary school. Early elementary school. In middle school she gave us *Speak* and *We Should All Be Feminists*. The parents of someone in my Girl Scout troop got upset when Mom talked about rape statistics while we were working on our self-defense badges. That was the end of my participation in Scouts. (Mainly because I was tired of being a cog in the machine of Big Cookie. But still.)

I throw my weight into grinding the spices. They don't need to be dust—they need to be cracked and bruised and flayed open. Like our family. I grind them to dust, then drown the spices in milk and water, setting the pot on the burner to heat up.

Mom's hunched over some college student's terrible analysis of *The Scarlet Letter* or *The Great Gatsby*, when what she studied—what she threw her heart into and went into grad school debt for—was the depiction of female vengeance in films made by men. And how the male gaze of one generation of filmmakers bleeds into the male gaze of the next generation—but not only filmmakers, because art reflects life.

Mom's life sent her down this path, the things that happened she doesn't talk about. The part of herself she keeps in darkness. From the sound of the note from her high school friend, it was a teacher. Maybe she had to write terrible papers on *The Scarlet Letter* for his class, hand them in, await his evaluation, his judgment on her voice.

A wave of nausea breaks over me and I grip the counter.

"Love?" She's there, hand on my cheek. "Are you all right?" She peers in the pot and turns the heat down. I always rush chai, when really it needs to simmer, give the flavors time to intermingle.

"You haven't been eating well. I don't think you're sleeping, either. Honey, maybe you should take a break from your writing project."

She thinks this is about Marguerite. "Yeah, okay. I will."

I want to ask her. I want to know this piece of her. Want her to know her story is worth telling. But also she doesn't owe it to me, or anyone. And if, after all these years of being a mother who was so open about all the ins and outs of womanhood, she hasn't chosen to tell us, asking would only hurt her all over again.

Will Nor tell her children? Her daughters? If she has them, someday when they're old enough to understand, if that's an age that ever comes, will she tell them or will they somehow one day wander upon some evidence, an internet post, maybe even one I wrote, and then Nor will be flayed open again.

AINSI TU SERAS

Emilde appears, helps Zahra
to her feet, then curtsies
as though my brother
is not clearly at my mercy.

> *Master Philippe*
> *my mistress asks for you.*

I keep pressure
on his throat.

Is Helene unwell?

> *She says*
> *only her brother*
> *can ease her worries.*

I release him.
The pure loathing
in his eyes would
flatten me if
I hadn't seen it
a million times before.
I move to follow him
but Emilde stops me.

> *Go. Helene*
> *will distract him.*
> *Go now.*

IN THE STABLE
I ask a question
Isabella cannot answer.

Am I a fool?

It matters not.
I won't be deterred.

> *You are a young woman*
> *of great conviction.*
>
> *And you have been wounded*
> *in such a way that only you*
> *know how to heal.*
> *If this is what you must do*
> *then no one shall stop you.*

WEAPONS AND ARMOR
to suit our frames
are concealed in packs
but Isabella insists
we have daggers
strapped against our thighs

> constant reminders
> of our power

and yet, now that
the moment is here
my limbs are lead.
What will this solve?
What will it change?

> *But, Marguerite.*

Isabella draws me aside.

> *I'll think no less of you*
> *if you decide*
> *against this path.*
> *There's more than one way*
> *to fight. You do not*
> *have to wield a sword.*

HELENE APPEARS
on silent footsteps
holding out her labor
of these many weeks.
It's folded over
larger than I realized.

Perhaps
everything about Helene
has always been larger
than I realized.

She unfurls the cloth,
a banner edged in silver tears
human bones and at the center

　　　　　an orange impaled
　　　　　on a lance.

The Prince of Orange.

Ainsi tu seras,
the script reads
both delicate and bold.

Thus shall you be.

I choke back a sob,
rush to embrace Helene
before remembering
she shrinks from touch.
But as I retreat, she
pulls me close, clings
to me like she never has before.

And Philippe?

A ghost of a smile
flits over Helene's face.

> *Locked in the cellar.*
> *Emilde stands guard.*

ON THE ROAD BEFORE DAWN:

        two girls
        once mistress, servant
        now comrades in arms

        two women who won't
        pass this way again
        but will complete
        what they set out to do.

CHAPTER THIRTY-ONE

I don't even like to ride the bus at night and Marguerite and Zahra are setting out into the unknown with only a few weeks of combat training and each other. What they'll find along the road could make up whole other books.

Maybe I'll write them, one day.

But this is the story I'm telling now. So what I choose to show has to be a piece of the bigger picture. Is every man they meet along the way a threat? Or could there be men who don't instill fear?

#notallmen and all that.

But they are a threat, unless proven otherwise. And two young women traveling alone don't have the luxury of allowing men to prove themselves trustworthy.

It wasn't just Craig.

It was the players and football fans who immediately rallied to support a water boy they'd never given the time of day to before, who thought the distraction to a football program was more damaging than the destruction of a girl's life.

It was the administration pledging a crackdown on the Greek system that fizzled the second the media looked away.

It was fraternity brothers who made him their pet, even though they hadn't considered him manly enough when he pledged. Because if he was guilty, what were they?

It was even running back Reece Hutchinson, hailed by feminist Twitter as the #notallmen hero we'd been waiting for because he testified on Nor's behalf, to the fury of the Husky faithful. He saw Nor and Craig together, saw how completely plastered she was. Saw Craig grabbing her arm and pulling her toward the back door. Even tried to stop them.

Didn't get drafted to the NFL, despite being a top-ranked prospect. But that's okay because at least he's a Twitter hero.

Except here's the thing: Reece Hutchinson is a human battering ram. Does anyone believe Craig Lawrence would have stood a chance against him? It didn't even have to get physical. If Hutchinson had done more than the barest minimum, had leveraged his status and done more than say, "Bro, maybe leave her alone," none of this would be happening.

Then, maybe, I'd consider him a hero. Except no one would know. And if no one applauds your feminism, did you even perform it?

PLEASE, SIR

A FULL DAY'S TRAVEL LATER
Zahra sinks into a hayloft
and she is gone to a land
I hope is more peaceful
than the one I visit
in my own dreams.

Sleep will not come for me
but the farmer will. I do not
block out Zahra's snores
the animal smells, my racing mind.
I pick hay from my stockings
                                        and wait.

Dependable as the goats
that must endure his rough hands
every morning, the farmer appears
silhouetted by the moon.

He scans the barn and
doesn't see us in the corner
where he said we could stay.

Finally he spots me leaning
over the edge of the hayloft.
I'm in no mood to hide.
He limps to the base of a ladder
in no condition to climb.

What you doing up there?

I smile at his frustration.

A girlish whim.

He retreats
to his safe, warm house,
no word of why
he came to the barn
in the dead of night.

We both know why.

ZAHRA AND I CREEP
from the barn
saddle our horses
and slink away
before the sun
has cracked the horizon.

What we will miss in breakfast
is worth avoiding what we will pay
in a thwarted farmer's anger.

PLEASE, MADAME.
My sister is with child,
her husband fallen in the war.
We travel to his village
so at least she may give birth
surrounded by his kin.

> *Please, monsieur.*
> *My cousin is unwell.*
> *If only you could see*
> *her mastery of womanly arts—*
> *she sings, she dances,*
> *she lifts the hearts of men.*
> *A bit of food might set her right*
> *and then . . .*

Please, Father,
we are lowly novitiates,
our convent overrun by scoundrels,
even our habits
ripped from our heads.
We only need
a place to rest
before we move on
to the Mother house.

Each time, a story
wilder than the last.

Each time, a meal,
some shelter, a bit of hope
to help us on our way.

Each time, my dagger at the ready.

WHAT IF HE'D ASKED
to see your womanly arts?

Zahra guffaws,
the ale we pinched
from our last benefactor
gone straight to her head.

We're close now.
By all reports we'll reach
de Gaucourt's camp by morning.

Didn't you know?
The duchess taught me
to waltz, as well as to kill.

No amount of ale
can distract us
from the truth
of what we have
set out to do.
I've had a taste—

       the man in the alley
       the man in the stable.

When the time comes
will I be capable
of draining the life
from a monster?

And do I want
that answer to be

       yes?

CHAPTER THIRTY-TWO

I write.

No one else can do this for me.

And this story has to be told. It can't be yet another folded-up scrap caught in the bottom of a shoebox.

I can't tell Nor's story. But I can tell Marguerite's. No one else is going to.

So I write, even when the sun is shining and I could be at Green Lake with Chester. I write, even when my dad asks me to help him make ravioli. I write, even when I miss a movie marathon with Mom, miss a Skype date with Francie and Sam, miss my grandma's birthday party.

I write, even when I could be sleeping except I couldn't really because my mind never stops spinning out the next piece of the story, Marguerite's story, the bedtime story we all should have heard but instead we got stories of princesses in towers and princes so inept they somehow got thorns in their eyes.

There's no prince to save Marguerite, just like there was no prince for Nor. Marguerite has to do this shit on her own, and she's scared—so am I—but she's not letting a little thing like abject terror stop her.

Marguerite knows how to wield a sword.

I will too before I'm done.

BINDINGS

Tents billow in the distance
resisting a wind that seeks
to tear them down.

Close enough we're almost there
but far enough they will not see us
stop, retreat behind some trees.

The trousers and tunics
borrowed from René
have served us well
as traveling clothes
but now we add the final detail:

> heavy linen strips
> to bind our breasts.

Because we're born
with the ability to produce food
and sustain life, we are considered
> weak.

I'd laugh if not for
the searing pain
as Zahra winds
the linen round my self.

Sᴇɴᴛʀɪᴇs ᴛʜʀᴏᴡɪɴɢ ᴅɪᴄᴇ
straighten up
at our approach.

I run a nervous hand
through close-shorn locks
then lift it in friendly greeting.
We wave the Crown's flag
but any sentry worth their sword
would know Chalon's men
are not above deceit.

I seek a deep breath
to steady my nerves
but my bindings only
allow the barest bit of air
into my lungs
and so my

CHAPTER THIRTY-THREE

It's bullshit.

Marguerite and Zahra having to cut their hair, bind their breasts, erase themselves.

It's my first impulse, born of *As You Like It* and *Twelfth Night* and *Lord of the Rings* and *Song of the Lioness*. Girls dressing as boys to gain access to what no one will give them otherwise. Only as boys can they possibly wield their rage.

The duchess would have advised it, probably. The cooler, calmer head prevailing. Sometimes you make sacrifices, play the game before you twist the rules.

But Marguerite doesn't have land and power, a duchy, a husband treating her as an equal, and a future with a girl she'll raise to be as fierce as she is. She's not operating from a place of security and support.

She's an untethered ball of rage.

The rules don't matter because she's never been playing a game.

And when she finds the Prince of Orange, she'll want him to know exactly who has come for him and why.

FLOWERS

Sᴇɴᴛʀɪᴇꜱ ᴛʜʀᴏᴡɪɴɢ ᴅɪᴄᴇ
straighten up
at our approach.

I run a nervous hand
through the length of my hair
then wave in friendly greeting.
We fly the Crown's flag
but any sentry worth their sword
would know Chalon's men
are not above deceit.

Zahra and I exchange a glance
then prod our horses forward
until we are right before the men.

Mesdemoiselles?

WE WISH TO SPEAK WITH
Governor de Gaucourt.

The taller of two sentries
chuckles, strokes Minuit's nose.

> *I doubt that will be necessary.*
> *If you have come to . . .*
> > *. . . meet the needs*
> *of our men at arms—*

We haven't.

A flicker of self-doubt.
Zahra argued we should use
assumptions to our advantage
if only to gain entry, but I refuse.

I do not judge the camp followers
who survive by men's basest desires
but I will not fall back on my form
when I have every right
to be here as I am.

The man's tone shifts.
Not only is my body
not for his pleasure but
I have interrupted him.

> *We have no need*
> *of cooks or washerwomen.*
> *You'd best be on your way.*

YOU MUST THINK US FOOLISH, SIRS.

Zahra giggles, setting out
on another story.
Will she say I'm addled,
with child, lovesick?

I won't wait to find out.
Waiting for someone else
to act is how we got here.

I'm almost sure
they won't run me through
with the nearest lance
when I force entry into the camp.

NOT SPEARED BUT GRABBED
the moment I'm in reach,
thrown hand to hand
and hauled into a tent
where terror chokes me.
If I had trusted Zahra—

Don't move.

The one left standing guard
is my age, maybe younger.

*I wish to speak
with the governor.*

I said, don't move!

He points his dagger
as though he'd use it.

I didn't threaten him.

I didn't draw my own dagger
tucked against the thigh
he'd never dream
could give him
anything but pleasure.
I only spoke.
Perhaps that's worse.

My traveling companion—

Shut your mouth!

I have to believe Zahra
is being held with more care.
She knows how to speak
to these men, she is not
blunt force like I.
But that is why
I will succeed.

THE YOUNG ONE IS
far too insecure,
too eager to prove
he's man enough.
The fact he's never
known a willing girl
only means he's sure to feel
entitled, enraged by any woman
who does not exist to please him.

He'd slice my throat
to show he could.

I wait until
he is replaced.

My new guard is weathered,
too old for this life
but he knows no other.
Nearly one hundred years
the battles for power have raged
and all anyone has to show
are dead brothers, sons,
the ones who live hardened,
desiring only to meet
their basest needs, survive.

CHAPTER THIRTY-FOUR

"Hon?"

Mom sticks her head in my door as though I haven't told her a million times to knock.

She waves a familiar blue box at me. "I got tampons."

"Okay? You can leave them on my dresser."

"Are you keeping some in here now?"

"Does it matter?" I slam my notebook shut.

"Of course not, sweetie, I just, I went to put them in your bathroom and saw that you still have a full box. I've run out, and we're usually pretty—"

"I didn't realize I had to account for every menstrual product I use now!"

I'm being a total brat and I'm fully aware of it but also incapable of stopping even when I see the pain written across Mom's face.

"I'm just worried about you."

"I'm not pregnant, if that's what you're suggesting," I say, jumping up and taking the box, then holding the door open in invitation.

"That wasn't what I was suggesting," she says, taking the unsubtle hint and walking through the door. "But if you were, you know you could—"

"Okay, thanks." I shut the door.

She thinks my systems are breaking down, that I'm not taking care of myself like I promised, that I'm not eating and sleeping and humaning like a normal person with normal worries who can afford to do those things, who has time and energy in their normal life because they don't have this story they have to tell bursting out of their chest like an alien, this story they have to keep telling or they'll never know how it turns out, if it turns out okay.

She's not wrong, either. But I don't care.

I NEED TO RELIEVE MYSELF.

My guard acts as though
he doesn't hear me
but the blush creeping
up his neck says otherwise.

Sir, if you please.
It's my time.

Still nothing.

I have the flowers.
The courses?
My flow is—

                Hold your peace!

He glances around
for someone to save him
from this most horrifying prospect—
a woman bleeding.

A DIVINE PUNISHMENT
on half the world
because one woman

      (as the story goes
      though let's be honest
      a woman didn't write that tale)

couldn't bear to pass up
a juicy piece of
      fruit:

The monthly shedding
of blood, without which
the wandering womb
would flood is capable of:

souring wine   felling fruit

    killing bees   blighting crops

infecting dogs   corroding male members

    killing children in the womb

    or should it live, poisoning a child
    through the vapors that flow
      through the eyes of a woman
        with the flowers.

So TERRIFYING, A WOMAN'S BLOOD,
but more terrifying still:

> A woman who does not bleed
> is prone to many forms of madness.
>
> And a woman who's mad
> is most terrifying of all.

ON YOUR FEET.

He jerks his chin to the door,
leads me on the point of his dagger
to a board suspended over a pit of waste.

My stomach turns.
In my rush to match
my mettle to any man's
I had not considered the reality
of day-to-day with soldiers.

Some privacy, sir?

The pit is situated
along the edge of the camp
backed up against scraggly woods.
If I were on my own, I could run for cover,
get a head start before he realized I'd gone.

But I didn't come
all this way to run
and most of all:

                    I'd never leave Zahra.

THE CAMP IS LAID OUT
as René predicted:
the grandest tent in the center,
home to the governor of Dauphine,
leader of these troops,
the only one with power
to let us stay as equals.

My captor is distracted
chatting with a fellow soldier
perhaps exchanging tips
on how best to protect their
crops and dogs and members
from the corrosion of a woman's flowers.

Do men discuss such things?

There's a chance
I can get from the pit
to the nearest tent
and from there decide
my next move.
A chance is all I need.

CHAPTER THIRTY-FIVE

What if I had a chance to be alone with Craig Lawrence and the dagger that's become an extension of my self? Only in the dead of night for now, safe inside my family home, but what if they became a reality, the scenes that play out on the movie screen of my mind once I've willed myself to sleep, fingers still gripped around the dagger's handle?

SUBSERVIENT

I MOVE AGAINST MY INSTINCT,
slowly, less prone to catch the eye.
The men continue talking,
avoiding me, my blood.

> (All the blood
> they spill on battlefields
> but one drop from my womb
> could bring them down.)

I reach the first tent,
heart in my throat.
My goal:
> find Zahra or
> reach the governor,
> whichever comes first.

WHEN SEVERAL MEN
stomp toward me
I fight the instinct to flee.
Instead, eyes down,
invisible, I play my role:
subservient woman who
cleans their soiled garments
cooks their meals
relieves them in the night.

They needn't know
she keeps a hand on the dagger
concealed beneath her skirts.

Emboldened when they pass
without a glance
I pick up my pace,
focus on reaching
the governor.

I'm very nearly there.
If I should shout
he'd probably hear
but shouting would draw
the wrong attention.
Head down
silent as thunder
I fight the urge to run
and then—

Mademoiselle de Bressieux?

CHAPTER THIRTY-SIX

Soft fingers intertwine with mine on cool, crisp sheets. Bright lights, anti-septic smell, a steady hum of voices and beeping, punctuated by calls over an intercom.

I'm back in the hospital with Nor, trying not to faint at the sight of her blood—they've stripped off her clothes while she stands in the middle of a sheet we have to hope will gather physical evidence, because god knows a girl's word isn't enough.

Except now I'm the one in a bed. My eyes drift down the length of my arm and land on the leather cuff encircling someone else's wrist.

Mom's only accessory is her simple wedding band.

I force my brain to do the work that's normally automatic, but under the haze of whatever they're pumping through me, it's a conscious effort to turn my head and see a sheet of jet-black hair falling over a face bowed low.

Jess is here. I manage to form words. "Are you praying?"

Their head snaps up. "Why, yes, yes I am. Praying to the goddess that you will survive so she can then smite you for reckless endangerment of my nerves!"

My brain isn't functional enough to wrap around Jess's words. "I'm fine." I squeeze their hand. At least I try. "You're here."

"In the flesh."

"I was such a jerk and you came from Saipan."

They laugh. "You were a total jerk. Terrible friend."

"Jess, I—"

"But I only came from San Francisco. And I was pretty shitty too, not responding to any of your messages or telling you where I'd gone."

"I saw a picture of you on a boat. With your mom."

Jess's brow furrows, then realization dawns. "Not my mom. Though if Dad has his way, she'll be my mom's replacement soon. That was Vanessa. In San Francisco Bay."

"You went with your dad?"

They shrug. "Mostly so I could go to a Guild of Cookery feast."

They ramble for a while about some young, medieval-obsessed chef duo that prepares eight-course meals in San Francisco based on period-correct recipes and cooking techniques.

That can't be the only reason they chose San Francisco over a tropical island, but who's to say how Jess's brain works. Whatever the reason, when I needed them, they were a short plane ride away. Even though I hadn't been there for them when I was only a couple miles away.

"How did you know . . . ?"

Jess waits, giving me a chance to articulate what happened. When I don't, they say, ". . . that you literally fell on your sword?"

"My sword?"

"Dagger, actually. But falling on one's dagger isn't a thing. Though turns out it can cause similar damage."

"I didn't fall . . ." At least I don't think so, but it's hazy what happened before I woke up here.

"You did eventually," Jess says. "They think you fainted at the blood. I realize I'm not the one who deserves sympathy here, but do you know how shitty I felt when your mom called me, asking if I knew how you'd gotten your hands on the deadly weapons under your bed?"

"My mom called you?"

"I was starting the third course of the feast: roast suckling pig, thank you very much, and sitting next to a lovely and charming silver fox named Antonio when my phone buzzed, and I wasn't going to answer it, but then I glanced at the screen and it was you, so how could I not? Because by that time you'd stopped trying to contact me, so of course I was desperate to hear from you. Only it was Kath."

"On my phone?"

"Not the pertinent detail here."

"She interrupted your special old-timey feast?"

"She didn't know. She still doesn't, so don't you dare tell her. I went straight to the airport."

I want to tell them they shouldn't have done that. That I'm sorry, for all of it. That I was an idiot for trying to master the rondel dagger because I'm a girl in a world where the knights can't be trusted and I don't deserve Jess and I'll make them all the suckling pig and pottage they want as soon as I'm out of here. At the very least, I'll go with them to the Medieval Faire out on the peninsula, and even wear a costume.

But I'm being pulled under yet again, so I squeeze their hand as my eyes drift closed.

———

The next time I wake, it's pitch-dark outside. I have no idea what time it was when Jess was here, but now it's Mom at my bedside, snoring softly in the uncomfortable hospital chair.

The fog of medicine is clearer now. I try to sit up, but my brain says no thank you. Back to the pillow I go. The thing is, I have to pee. When Nor was recovering from a burst appendix in seventh grade, a catheter allowed her to stay in bed while her urine collected in a bag at her side. She thought it was revolting but I thought it was the coolest thing ever.

I don't have a catheter, as far as I can tell. That seems like a good sign. It's slowly coming back to me now—Marguerite confronted by a soldier who recognizes the crest on her ring, dagger at the ready, my own rondel at my side, in my hand, protecting Marguerite, Elinor, my mother—

I don't want to bother Mom, but I also don't really want a strange nurse helping me pee—and I think the ship has kind of sailed on bothering my parents.

"Mom?"

I barely whisper, but the second I've spoken, she's on her feet. "I'm awake! I'm up! Marianne? Sweetheart? Are you okay?"

"I have to pee."

The look on her face morphs from severe anguish to slight confusion to a mixture of relief and amusement. "Okay, pee. I'll call for a nurse."

She reaches for the call button, but I stop her. "Can't you take me?"

"Oh. Okay." She brushes hair off my forehead. "Sure honey. We can manage that."

I've never wanted peeing to be a joint activity, but if I have to do it with someone, better my mother than anyone else, I guess. She helps me sit up slowly and pivot my legs off the side of the bed. With each movement my entire right thigh screams.

"Nice and slow," Mom coos.

My bladder isn't going to wait. I sling an arm around her shoulder and let her hoist me to my feet. I thought my thigh hurt before. I let out a moan and Mom drops me back down, which doesn't exactly help.

"I am going to wet the bed," I say through gritted teeth. "Please."

We try again and this time make it the few feet to a room barely bigger than an airplane bathroom. There are convenient handrails all around and another call button for the nurses' station in here as well. Because I guess not everyone has their mom at their side when they suffer a self-inflicted medieval dagger wound.

Mom settles me on the toilet and squats down in front of me, ready to catch me if I should topple off. It's sort of the most vulnerable thing in the world to pee like this, with her right here, but it's also sort of okay? She's my mom—she grew me inside of her, washed my diapers, changed my peed-on sheets. She got bloodstains out of the white skirt I was wearing the first day of seventh grade when I got my period.

We've shared everything. Except that she left out one huge part of her life, her experience of being a woman. Which she didn't owe me, but at the same time, if we had known, maybe it would have changed things somehow. Maybe Nor would have made another choice, maybe I would, maybe . . .

———

The next time I wake, both Mom and Papi are there and bright sunshine streams through the windows.

"Hola, mija," Papi says, leaning over to kiss me on the forehead. "Jess sends their love."

Mom's still on the chair where I guess she slept the night, her skin ashen and the circles beneath her eyes an alarming shade of gray.

No Nor.

"When can I go home?" I ask. Papi sits on the edge of the hospital bed and I try not to wince at the searing pain in my leg.

"Hopefully today," he says. "They need you to talk to one more doctor this morning, and if all goes well, vamos para la casa."

"Just talk?"

Mom shifts in the chair, clearly agitated. "Go on and tell her, Andrés. Better she be prepared."

Papi sighs. "It's a psych evaluation."

I thought my brain was clearer this morning. I even jotted a few notes on where I left off: Marguerite comes face-to-face with the man she's been betrothed to since she was twelve. A good man, but not good enough to understand what she could possibly be doing in the camp of the king's army.

Still, I can't quite put it all together. Some of it came back in pieces through the night when I woke up to change position, take a pill. Frantic between the dagger and the pen, working out how Marguerite would protect herself, face-to-face with someone who could ruin everything. She'd be outmatched in brute strength, but not cunning and agility. She could wield a dagger as an extension of herself, she could send it slicing through the air until—

"They have to make sure you're not a danger to yourself," he says more softly.

I blink at him. "A danger . . . ?"

Mom rubs her face. "It's not generally the most well-adjusted individuals who stab themselves with a medieval sword worth thousands of dollars."

"Kath."

Mom stands abruptly. "Sorry. I'm going to get some coffee."

She doesn't return. Papi's the one who stays with me when the psychiatrist comes, tablet in hand, less warm and fuzzy therapist than clinician checking off boxes to absolve the hospital of liability if I get out and impale myself more effectively the next time.

I try to stay calm. That's the whole point—to show them I'm mentally stable. I wasn't trying to kill myself. Or even hurt myself. There was an accident. And blood, apparently, and I passed out.

But it's almost like she's trying to press my buttons. Maybe she is. She brings up Nor's case and the notorious video—*I feel like learning how to use a fucking sword*; she wants to know where I got the weapons. I don't see how that matters until I realize she's hinting they might be stolen.

But I don't want to get Jess in trouble.

Finally I lose my temper. "First of all, it was a dagger, not a sword. And if I was trying to kill myself, wouldn't I have gone an easier route than stealing antique weapons and trying to impale myself?"

She doesn't rise to the bait. "So they are stolen?"

"They belong to her friend, Jess," Papi interjects. "I believe Marianne was storing the weapons for her friend."

Coming out of someone else's mouth, I realize how dumb that sounds. *It's not my weed, Mom! I was holding it for a friend!* But my parents know Jess and they know me, and they trust us both. At least they did until now.

There are more questions, but finally, with follow-up appointments scheduled and pain medications prescribed, we're on our way home.

T BIAS

HIS IS HIGHLY IMPROPER—

*I must speak
with the governor.*

Ismidon de Primarette
is flustered
by the girl
before him.

The twelve-year-old
he was betrothed to
was unpolished, wild,
but surely I've been refined
in his years away?

*I have traveled
from the duchy of Anjou
and before that
the convent at Salette
and before that
my own home
which is now a morgue
filled with rotting bodies
of my parents and our household.
Our families are meant to be allies.
I must speak with the governor.*

AN AIDE DISPATCHED
to locate Zahra,
de Primarette leaves
to locate the governor.
It seems he does not want
to parade me through the camp.

The horror.

For once
I do as I am told
and sit, wait, hope
I have not been a fool
to trust this man.

At least no more a fool
than every person
in this camp
who forsakes the comforts
of home, their family's peace
of mind, to chase victory
in a war that has no end.

ZAHRA SOBS
and falls
into my arms.

Her escort sighs,
these feeble women.

Zahra had been stranded
outside the camp, no word
of where I'd been taken
and no assurance
she'd ever see me again.

I wipe her tears.
She wipes mine.

Chin up now.
We cannot let them
see us cry.

The moment a man
senses weakness
in a woman

> a creature he already
> judges as weak
> even though she bears
> the children, the weight
> responsibility for all
> evil in the world

he only finds
his bias confirmed.

CHAPTER THIRTY-SEVEN

Chester jumps on me before I'm all the way inside.

"Fuera, chucho," Papi says, shooing him away.

I kind of want to throw my arms around Chester, the only one with no opinions on my dagger injury, but it hurts to lean down and pet him.

"Couch or bed?" Papi asks, his hand gentle on my elbow.

"Her bed is a mess," Mom says from the kitchen table, where I'm startled to see her sitting with Jess. I don't know where else I thought Jess would be, since neither of their parents is in town and they came back to Seattle because of me.

I crumple on the couch while Papi heads to clear off my bed. I can't remember what's on it—scrapbook stuff or Marguerite stuff—but at least it's Papi and not Mom. Chester jumps up and settles at my feet, his breath steady and warm—Chester, my hound, my constant.

Jess sits on the floor next to the couch. "You got the all clear?"

"Just a flesh wound," I say.

"It's not a joke." Mom doesn't fawn over me.

"Your sister said she'd come by later," Jess says, glancing briefly toward my mom.

"You talked to Nor?"

"We've been texting a little. She has class until four."

At least she hasn't forgotten me, isn't angry with me, like Mom. Not angry enough to completely ignore me, anyway.

"Aside from the flesh wound, how are you feeling?"

"I'm okay. Sore."

"Who would have thought?" Mom says. "That if you stabbed yourself with a medieval sword, you might be a touch sore!"

I don't think pointing out that it was a dagger is the right move here. Thankfully Jess reads the room as well.

"But I'm so glad to hear you're feeling fine," she goes on. "The rest of us are just peachy too."

Chester sits up, ears cocked, considering Mom's strange vocal register. Probably the other dogs in the neighborhood do too.

"Since everyone's feeling so excellent, maybe now's a good time to discuss this!" She holds up something I hadn't noticed on the kitchen table in front of her.

My notebook. A rusty smear across the cover.

Her bed is a mess.

"You went through my stuff?"

Now she gets up and heads my way, but I don't think she plans to stroke my hair. "Oh, excuse me if I put a few things away when I was scrubbing the giant bloodstain on your carpet!"

Jess scrambles to their feet between us, putting up an appeasing hand. "She didn't, though. She didn't find the notebook in your stuff. I showed it to her."

"Thank you, Jess," Mom says. "I really appreciate all you've done. Would you give us some privacy now, please?"

"Yes, ma'am." *Ma'am?* Jess throws me an apologetic look and heads down the hall, going into Nor's room.

"Nor's room?"

"Absolutely none of your concern," Mom snaps. Then she pinches the bridge of her nose and takes a slow, steady breath. When she's done, the manic gleam in her eye is unchanged, but she pulls a chair closer to the couch and sits, gripping the notebook in both hands. Marguerite.

"We talked about this."

"Mom—"

"No, you know what? I'm going to talk now. I try to listen. I try to be the kind of mom who listens. Sometimes I screw it up, but most of the time I think I do a pretty decent job—"

"You do—"

Death glares stop me in my tracks. "And all that listening sometimes means I don't get my say. I have plenty of opinions about your choices, Nor's choices. Don't think I don't. But I bite my tongue until it's raw because you're your own young women and I'm trying to let you make the mistakes you have to make to grow, but sometimes you're Chester sticking your nose under that fence, asking to get scratched!"

She takes a shuddery breath as Papi steps into the room. "So I'm speaking my piece now. You'll have your turn."

Which is honestly kind of a relief, to know that no one's expecting any explanations from me right now.

She holds up Marguerite. "We talked about this. We talked about how it was upsetting you. Of course I want you to express yourself. Of course I believe in the power of story. You can judge the books I teach so there's food on our table, but you're not the only one who loves stories around here! The difference is I want our family to be able to move on and I don't know how we do that if we keep rehashing this one event!"

This one event. Like it was a piano recital or a house fire.

"If all you were doing was expressing yourself creatively, well okay then. But, Marianne, my love, you stabbed yourself. After you were televised telling the whole world you wanted to learn how to use a fucking sword."

"I wasn't going to hurt myself. Or anyone else! It was research!"

"I don't care." She's the worst liar in the history of the world. She cares like Marguerite cares, like Duchess Isabella cared when she rode into battle herself to rescue René from men holding him for ransom. Like Isabella's daughter Margaret of Anjou cared when she ruled all of England in place of her mad husband, so pissing off the men with her power that they disinterred her remains and scattered them during the French Revolution.

That's life for a woman who won't shut up.

"I'm keeping this for now," Mom says, holding my notebook close. "You need to rest. Clearly we need to get you some counseling. Jess explained about the swords and your father is going to lock them in the shed with his tools. That's all I have to say right now."

She gets up and heads toward the hall, taking all my research, words, heart with her.

"How'd that work out for you?" I could control myself, but I don't. "Keeping silent. Stuffing it down. Not telling anyone about what happened to you. Super healthy, right?"

"I don't know what you're talking about." She's almost reached her bedroom door.

"How about Marla? Does Marla know?"

She stops, her shoulders tense. I'm right, I can see it. She never told anyone else. Maybe not even Papi. My mom, who took me to endless marches as a kid, waving signs that said I WILL NOT BE SILENCED.

"And that teacher? Your silence worked out pretty well for him, I'm guessing. How about the girls he hurt after you were gone?"

Her face echoes that night when she arrived at the emergency room and couldn't process what the doctors were telling her, but then I stepped out of Nor's exam room into the hall and she realized we would never be the same again.

I can't explain my fury with her, that she didn't tell me, because I know she doesn't owe me. I've done enough reading about survivors to know they get to control who they tell, that they don't have to tell anyone, that not everyone is safe enough or wants the scrutiny, I know all this. But also, decay thrives in darkness.

Just like *Lady Snowblood* becomes *Kill Bill*, Toshiya Fujita passes a legacy to Quentin Tarantino, Mom's abuser hands his privilege to Craig Lawrence. And we all let it happen, every one of us.

Mom chokes out a sob and her door slams behind her.

I almost wish I could take it back.

CHAPTER THIRTY-EIGHT

I can't take it back.

I've made such a mess of so many things, and before the hospital, before the blood, there was Marguerite, sneaking through the Royalist camp, recognized yet again by her father's ring.

I've left her there, huddled with Zahra. At the mercy of a man who might have been an ally when her family could have increased his power. She has no family anymore. She is no longer an advantage and she has no reason to trust Ismidon de Primarette.

I can't make things better with my mom, but I can do something for Marguerite.

I can give her someone worth trusting. This man, Ismidon de Primarette, her betrothed from the time she was twelve, can be someone who may not understand her fight but will try to help anyway. Who'll put his own reputation on the line to get her an audience with the governor. The governor, who won't just let her fight, that would be too easy, but she's not taking no for an answer.

Mom can take my notebook—the one Papi gave me for expressing myself—but it's not going to stop me from telling this story.

Just like one arrogant, shortsighted army commander isn't going to keep Marguerite and Zahra from doing what they set out to do.

ARMOR

H E WILL NOT
even look me
in the eye

directing his scorn
to Ismidon instead.

> *They may stay.*
> *They'll cook or clean*
>
> *unless*
> *they'd rather serve*
> *the men in other ways.*

To service men
with our bodies
would be appropriate.

To speak
our minds:
obscene.

THE TWO WOMEN
who must share
their cramped space
are displeased but
their irritation wanes
as they realize
we are to relieve
their burdens.

But we have no intention
of washing soiled braies.

> *I am Zahra,*
> *this is Madem—*

Marguerite.
I am Marguerite.

The older one sighs
picks up a bucket
and leaves the tent.
The younger studies us.

> *You are her servant?*

She directs the question
to Zahra, but I answer.

We're sisters.

SISTERS AS WE BIDE OUR TIME
serving slop to soldiers
sleeping with men on all sides
piling hair into helmets
that shield our faces

and sisters as we make our way
with the swagger of those
born into privilege
to where the others
swing their swords
in a melee meant to train

or maybe fool themselves
into believing that when faced
with lance or spear or battle ax
they will not soil themselves
faint dead away or throw
their arms up in surrender.

YOU THERE!

A dark-skinned officer,
young but confident,
points our way as
we approach.

>   *You'll spar with him.*

He jerks his thumb
toward a beast of a man.
My heart stutters but
this is what I came for.
I step forward.

>   *Not you, him.*

He wants Zahra.
Zahra, barely trained,
here for loyalty,
friendship, love.
She would not be
the first to die in training.

She knows it.
She steps forward.

CHAPTER THIRTY-NINE

Chester barks when Nor arrives, the joyful bark he does for her and no one else. That's the only sound that cuts through the white noise blasting in my ears.

I stay in my room, even when I hear Jess and Nor laughing together, smell chicken soup and home-baked bread.

When Nor comes to my door—hours later, I think, but time passes strangely when writing a battle, the moments between a lifted blade and the strike that ends a life interminable and also over before you've had a chance to consider what it means to kill—I pretend I'm asleep.

She comes in anyway, sits on the edge of my bed, strokes my hair.

"Sometimes," she whispers, "sometimes it feels like this gaping wound is never going to heal. If we cover it up, it never gets sunlight. If we leave it uncovered, it gets infected. The body has all these amazing ways to heal itself. But what happens when that's not enough?"

She stays for a long time. I think she cries.

COUNTERSTRIKES

CANNOT BEAR
to watch, yet
will not leave her.

Zahra's opponent
is on the offensive
from the jump.
His first few blows
make him overconfident.

But Zahra's lack of training
makes her unpredictable
and her size, agile.

A circle of men
forms, attracted by
her unusual style.

Who is that?

Dunno.

Little guy . . .

Impressive, though . . .

A sword clatters
to the ground
and Zahra stands,
grip still firm
on her own blade,
pointing it calmly
at her opponent's throat.

THE ONLOOKERS EXPLODE
in good-natured jeers
toward the fallen man
who Zahra helps up,
a show of chivalry.

The officer steps forward,
claps Zahra on the shoulder.

> *Well done, son.*
> *You still a squire?*

If Zahra responds
her voice is muffled
by her helmet, her visor.
I think that a blessing
until—

    he reaches out

        flips up her visor

           and freezes.

THE MAN SHE BESTED
lunges, sword at her throat.

Reveal yourself!

He roars as though
she were an English soldier.

The men around me
explode again—

confusion.

With trembling hand
my sister removes her helmet.

BEFORE HE CAN REACT
my sword is at his throat.

She's neither squire
nor knight, but maid
who bested you
on level ground.

Livid voices join in protest.
The young officer steps between
the enraged foot soldier
and the interloper.

Let's take a moment—

The officer is shoved aside.

This isn't a playground
for little girls.

She wasn't playing
when her sword
was on your neck.

I flip up my own visor.

Release her.
I challenge you.

THIS MAN THINKS
because of his sex
he is entitled
to win every game
every battle
no matter the stakes
death or pride
and I have a few things
to teach him
because despite
all their learning
there are quite a few
lessons boys still need
to learn.

AN IMPOSSIBLE CHOICE:

accept my challenge
and legitimize me

or

show his fear
of being bested by a girl.

Again.

THESE MEN
know nothing
of impossible
choices.

He cannot back down
and besides he is certain
he'll grind me to dust
make his point
erase the image
of Zahra's sword
at his throat
in the minds of the men
he calls his brothers.

He shoves Zahra away,
turns his sword on me.

He's enraged.
But his spark of fury
is nothing to my all-consuming fire.

BE AGGRESSIVE, MARGUERITE.

Isabella's voice
drifts through my mind
and somewhere further back
my father's.

> *Take the initiative!*
> *Displace his blows*
> *with counterstrikes—*
> > *he will not see you coming.*

Lessons in technique
flee for cover like birds
startled by the clash
of weapons in their meadow.

> *Counter the blows*
> *with your edge*
> *against his flat.*

The short version
of all the drills
and repetition,
techniques and theory?

Try not to die.

Metal on metal—

blade on blade
or doors once thought secure
wrenched open
a fortress breached
a life destroyed.

Either way
I'll show this monster
what a woman can do.

MY BRIGANDINE'S
quilted leather
is not enough
to stop the blade
slicing my forearm.

My howl is not
for the gash in my flesh
but the rage that a man
has once again
shoved his blade
in what is mine.

Wounded animal
enraged woman
trained soldier

it no longer
matters
who I am
only that I fight.

AFTER I DISARM HIM
I would gladly
take off his head
if not stopped
by the officer
who looks at me
with something
approaching respect.

Peace.
You are the victor.

The men around us
thrum with fury.
Perhaps our journey
ends right here.

But then:

What's this?
Our very own
Maid of Orléans?

Governor de Gaucourt
arrives to lend authority
to his young officer,
stepping neatly between
their swords and our necks.

Is your passion
divinely inspired,
demoiselle?

A few men snicker.
I keep my head down.

No sir.
I merely wish
to fight.

> *And where*
> *did a noble girl*
> *learn to fight?*

My father taught me.
The Duchess of Anjou
made me a warrior.

> *Ah yes, Isabella.*
> *Remarkable form, she has.*

Chortles from the men.

> *And your servant?*
> *The duchess taught her too?*

Zahra is my partner.
Together we are unstoppable
as your men can attest.

I jerk my chin
toward the miserable
heap on the ground
stanching the flow
of blood from his nose
with his sleeve.

Do you really think
you have the stomach
to end a life?

Fury rises.
These bodies of ours
he thinks so weak
are capable of creating life
slaughtering it for supper.
Blood flows from our wombs
over and over
and still we rise
to face another day
create more life
slaughter it
live on.

CHAPTER FORTY

I write into the early morning, skipping my pain pills to keep my mind clear. No amount of narcotics could make me forget the things I said to my mom, but Marguerite makes me forget everything but the blade in her hand.

Every minute I don't have pen to paper, the pages of my mind fill up with what will happen next, drafts so rough they're more feelings than words. Her brother will track her to the camp, making everything about himself, picking a fight with Ismidon, berating his sister. But Marguerite will prove herself to the governor, and the governor runs this show. Instead of bringing his runaway sister to heel, Philippe will be sent away with his tail between his legs.

I sleep only when I know Marguerite has a path to the battlefield.

I don't get up until I know the house will be empty. But I've forgotten about Jess until I see them staring into a teacup at the kitchen table. Then it surges back: They told Mom about my writing. Not only told her, but showed her the notebook. And now they're apparently living in Nor's room.

"So have you replaced my sister, or what?"

Jess's head jerks back like I slapped them.

"I know your own family is pretty shitty, but I've got to say, this one isn't much of an improvement."

They shake their head. "I can see how it might be super oppressive to have parents who care that you exist."

I'm not getting into Oppression Olympics with Jess. For one thing, I'd lose, and it's not a game you want anyone to win. But it doesn't change the fact that they completely betrayed me.

I grab the smaller cast-iron pan and set it on the burner to heat up. Then I yank the refrigerator open, sending the salad dressing and assorted condiments in the door sprawling on their shelf. I grab the eggs and leave the chaos of bottles for whoever comes along next.

"You had no right to give my mom my book."

"Our book?"

"No." I crack an egg. "My book. That you were doodling on." Another egg.

"Doodling? Wow."

They want me to jump in and tell them it's their book too. That's what Nor would do. "Look, Jess—"

"No, I get it. It's all about you. It always has been. But what are you even writing this for? Therapy? You're the one championing how we have to tell these stories, different stories. But if it's only ever for you, then what's the point?"

"I know you're invested—"

"I am invested, and don't be condescending. It's possible I might relate to the fear of moving through the world in a body that's not the default."

You are absolutely not my type, princess.

What Jess has given me is so much more than doodling. Even if they'd never put ink to paper. But I'm still furious.

"Why would you tell my mom, knowing how she'd react?"

"First of all, I didn't know how she'd react! Parents who care what's going on with their kids are not my area of expertise! But you had injured yourself. Badly! We were all trying to understand what happened. Have you given any thought to what that must have been like for Kath? To find you in a pool of your own blood? And how much worse it would have been if she hadn't found you right away?"

If it had been Jess in the pool of blood, their parents wouldn't have found them right away. Or maybe not at all. I grab a bell pepper from the fridge, scrambling to keep the salad dressing from falling out because some asshole left it toppled over last time they closed the door.

"I wasn't trying to hurt myself."

"I believe you. But either way, you needed help. You were spiraling. I know I'm self-absorbed sometimes, but I was worried—I *am* worried—so when your sobbing mother asked me if I knew why you'd impaled yourself in your bedroom, I was not going to lie to her!"

The fact that they're right only makes me double down on my absurdly shifting ground. If I let myself think about Mom finding me like that, knowing what her face looked like the night Nor was attacked, then I can't be furious at her for lying to me.

Is it a lie if she never told me her story? After a lifetime of championing the importance of stories?

"You're a real hero, Jess. A model child who I'm sure my parents would be delighted to adopt. You can move into Nor's room, since she's clearly never coming back. But I'll take it from here with Marguerite."

"You wouldn't even know about Marguerite without me!"

"You're right. How can I ever make it up to you? But I did the work. I did the research. I literally bled for this story."

"I have been at your side, right up until you shoved me away. Now I have no part in it? Doing it alone doesn't make you strong, Marianne, it makes you stupid. It makes you fucking Philippe, running wild all over the countryside with no chance of accomplishing anything for the people you love!"

"You're comparing me to Philippe?"

"Stings, doesn't it? When you fancy yourself Marguerite. I can see how you'd take offense, he's such an asshole, because all the men are! He keeps chasing her down just so you can prove how much better she is. He's lost his entire family too, you know."

"How are you sympathizing with Philippe?"

"It's not even subtle, he's nowhere in the historical record. You went out of your way to add yet another douche-bro to your story because your tunnel vision—"

"I had to make him up! I made Helene up too! There's no record of Marguerite's family!"

"That's what happens when a person doesn't exist!"

At first I think it's another weapon meant to slice into me again because we're angry and we're hurling daggers, but when I throw a disparaging glance their way, I see a truth in their eyes, a chill.

"Wait, what?"

"Do a little poking around on genealogy websites. Look beyond what you want to find. It's not that hard to see that the Bressieux line died out before Marguerite was born. She's a legend. No more historical than the Lady of the Lake."

I grasp for something to hold on to, my dagger, and I find the handle of the cast-iron pan. I gasp at the searing pain, but also I focus on it. Burning flesh is nothing to the thought that I've built everything on shifting sand, mere stories.

CHAPTER FORTY-ONE

The stairwell of Nor's apartment building still smells like weed and rat poison, but there's also the distinct aroma of a simmering tomato sauce.

When Wyatt opens the door, the smell wafts over me even stronger. "Hey, Marianne! Come on in!"

"Hey."

"Come on in here, girl!" calls Tonika. "Do you have the Morales culinary touch? Because this sauce still needs something but I can't figure it out."

Tonika grins and holds out a ladle when I step into the kitchen.

I take it, even though I definitely don't have the Morales culinary touch. But Tonika's right. The sauce is more than a little bland. "I'm not sure," I say. "Nor would know."

Tonika takes the ladle back. "Your sister's at the pool and she's taking her sweet time."

"Wait . . ." The word *sweet* jogs my memory. "Sugar! Not very much, like a teaspoon. It's to cut the acidity of the tomatoes."

It had been a huge argument between Papi and Nor one late summer afternoon a few years back, when they were using up all the tomatoes in the garden for a sauce they planned to distribute to anyone who would take a jar.

Papi argued that tomatoes are naturally sweet and he hardly believed Sicilian grandmas were adding white sugar to their heirloom recipes. Nor argued that the sweetness can get cooked out of the tomatoes as they simmer, and a touch of sugar would bring that natural sweetness back while also cutting the acidity.

Mom and I stayed out of it. My favorite part of any dish that involved tomato sauce was always the pasta or bread, anyway.

Finally Nor and Papi split the sauce they'd made into two different pots. Nor added sugar to hers. Papi's confidence waned as Nor carried on happily, while his sauce was clearly not meeting his own standards.

When they were ready, Nor felt Mom and I would be too biased as taste testers (though I don't know who she thought we'd favor). So they each took a bowl of their sauce and a handful of spoons outside, where our neighbors, the Bianchis, caroused in their backyard dining area. (Complete coincidence that they happened to be Italian, but it was a fact Nor would not let Papi forget in years to come.)

The Bianchis were happy to be consulted, and the spoons and bowls of sauce were passed across the fence with no explanation of the difference between them—only the assignment to taste test and report back.

Papi has included sugar in his tomato sauce ever since.

"Have you seen this place on Latona?" Wyatt asks from behind a screen. "Three bedrooms, plus a walk-in closet."

"Are you gonna sleep in the closet?" Tonika asks, emerging from the cupboard with a canister of sugar.

"Are you guys moving?"

"We weren't going to." Tonika adds a teaspoon to the sauce. "But we don't want to kick Nor out when Lola gets back. So we're looking for a place that'll fit us all."

My face must betray something, because Tonika adds, "Oh shit, I hope I didn't tell you something Nor wanted to tell you on her own. Nothing's for sure."

Nothing's ever for sure. And I don't actually hate the idea of Nor living off campus anymore. Tonika's great and Wyatt seems cool enough. If Nor is happy with them, I guess that's all I really need to know.

Not that it's up to me.

Tonika holds out the ladle again and I taste. We both nod at the same time. "Perfect, right?" she says. "You do have the Morales touch! Just like your sister!"

Which prompts me to burst into tears, right there in the middle of this crappy college student kitchen.

"Whoa, hey, what is happening?" Tonika drops the ladle in the sauce and leads me over to the kitchen table. She snaps her fingers in Wyatt's face. "You, tea, now."

Obedient, he hops up and starts filling a kettle.

"What's up, baby sis?"

I glance over at Wyatt. I don't know Tonika any better than I know Wyatt, I guess, but still—

Tonika jerks her thumb over her shoulder. "Does that boy need to make himself scarce?"

He freezes, unsure whether he should keep making the tea or get out of the kitchen. But Nor feels safe here, so Wyatt must be okay.

"No," I say, sniffling. "This is your house. I'm just a mess."

"You sure are," Tonika says. "Me too. Wyatt's the biggest mess of all of us."

Suddenly I'm telling them about this story I've been writing and the pointlessness of it and then it turns into telling them about Jess and how horrible I've been to this person who's been right by my side all summer, who has their own reason to care deeply about Marguerite's story. They let me talk, nodding and offering supportive sounds.

When I'm finally quiet, Tonika says to Wyatt, "Remember that time I made you swear not to let me drink at that Kappa Sig party and you found me with a drink in my hand and gently reminded me of my own wishes?"

Wyatt grins. "It wasn't the first time I've had a drink poured on me, but it was the first time I definitely didn't deserve it."

I take a shuddery breath.

"We're all assholes to the people we love sometimes," Wyatt says to me.

"You own it," Tonika says. "And you do better the next time."

They're a family, this odd assortment of people who've moved their garage sale furniture in together and built a home where they take in strays and screw up and forgive and keep muddling through the mess of living in relationship with one another.

A key clicks in the front door and Nor comes around the corner with wet hair and a gym bag over her shoulder. She pauses when she sees me, takes in my red, teary face, the tea in front of me, Tonika's gaze trying to beam whole paragraphs of concern into Nor's head via an exchanged look.

"Em? What's wrong?"

"It's stupid," I say.

"No, it's not," Wyatt says.

Tonika grabs my hand and gives it a squeeze. "You've got this." She jerks her head at Wyatt and they both disappear into her room.

Nor holds up her car keys. "Want to get out of here?"

I haven't been inside Nor's car since before.

It's been her one constant, from house to dorm to apartment, always she's had Uncle Joel's hand-me-down car. Even though the locks have never worked and the rear window is cracked, maybe the familiarity somehow feels safe.

The car's smell of chlorine tickles the back of my throat, ever-present reminder of what Nor has lost, but also of summers at the community pool, Nor flinging herself into the deep end before she'd even learned to swim and somehow figuring it out while I clung to the edge.

Sometimes she's the brazen one. I still can't swim.

She rolls the windows down and turns the music up. KEXP is doing yet another Kurt Cobain retrospective. I don't know where we're going and it doesn't even matter. I've fucked this all up so enormously but she's still here. She's still my sister.

We end up at the Fremont Troll. It's been years since we've been here, back before Nor could drive, when we used to ride our bikes to this massive art installation, an eighteen-foot troll statue under a bridge near our house. Like no time has passed, we climb the troll together, helping each other up over the hand crushing a real VW Bug, and scaling the troll's shoulder, where we perch together.

"I talked to Jess," Nor finally says. "And before you get mad at them, Mom was worried about what was going on between you two and I'm the one who reached out. If it helps, they feel terrible."

"For what?" The cars on the bridge above us rumble by, each one a self-contained world of people with their own fears and wounds and joys. "For telling me the truth?"

Nor is quiet for a minute. "You guys were really serious about this story, huh?"

Story. The word crushes me like the troll's hand on the puny car below us. It was always only a tale. Legend or history, it was never going to change anything.

"It was me being stupid. Making things my business that weren't. Thinking I could tell someone else's story, like that way I could make it end how it should."

"Wouldn't that be something?" Nor says. "If by telling a story you could change history."

A couple of tourists appear, reading the plaque about the troll. In 1989, the Fremont Arts Council held a competition for proposals to rehabilitate the area under the bridge, which had become a haven for drug dealers. Changing the story with art.

1989. Right around the time my mom was a student at Fremont High and there was a teacher who knew he could take what he wanted from a girl. Only that's not my story, either.

"Do you mind if we take a picture?" One of the tourists calls to us, holding up their phone.

"No problem," Nor calls back. "We'll climb down."

"No, stay!" the other one calls. "It'll show how massive it is."

Nor's had enough cameras in her face. "You can climb off," I tell her. "I'll stay."

"It's okay." She gives a friendly wave to the tourists to go ahead. "They have no idea who we are."

Nor drops her head onto my shoulder, a mass of curls falling in front of her face. I plaster on fake cheer for the photo.

This monumental thing that changed our lives, shoved us under a microscope, was barely a blip on the radar for the rest of the world. Even the rest of Seattle. Fremont. It was one girl, one family, an invisible fallen soldier in a war that has no end.

When the tourists have gone back to their bike-shares, Nor sits up and says, "I don't think you're telling someone else's story, though. Or trying to change history to suit what you want. For one thing, Marguerite didn't leave any record of who she was or how she'd want her story told. Or if she did, it was erased by those with power. You're illuminating, not erasing.

"You're going to mess up. You're not perfect, and neither was she. But I think you're trying your best to honor her story. And mine." Nor takes my hand. "Ultimately, I think you're telling a story about sisters. And violence. And being a girl in the world. That *is* your story to tell."

Maybe. But the existence of records or not and what that means won't leave me alone. All those baby pictures of Nor and hardly any of me. If some historian tried to reconstruct my life years from now, would they see the lack of photos as an indication that I never existed? Or would they see the lack as evidence of a second child and harried parents and do the work to build the character they hoped I was? Would I even want that? So much would depend on who was doing the telling.

"What if the lack of records means it never happened? Then what am I doing?"

"Writing a novel?" Nor grins and nudges my shoulder. "This is about the genealogy, yeah? Jess told me it suggests the Bressieux line died out."

"Right before Marguerite was born," I say. "Supposedly born."

Nor is quiet for a moment. "Who's the villain in the story?"

Chalon. De Gaucourt. Philippe. Every single person with power who built a world we can't walk through safely. "Louis de Chalon, I guess. The Prince of Orange."

"Any doubt about whether he existed?"

"No, he was real."

"How are you sure?"

"There's . . . history. Documentation. Of marriages, births, deaths. Battles. His existence is really well-established."

"Huh."

"What?"

"Well, who writes the history books?"

At first I think she's asking, like, specifically, who authored the books I read for research. But then I see the glint in her eye that suggests she's hoping for a certain answer.

"It's power again," she finally says. "It's always power. So it's not especially surprising that no one questions the villain's existence. With Marguerite's family, something tells me not every single person's name got recorded. Doesn't the 'family line' mean male heirs? The ones who inherited the titles? So if her loser brother got killed in one of those battles, maybe the Bressieux line did die out? Doesn't have to mean she didn't exist."

A flicker of light in the darkness. I can't even articulate why it matters so much to me that she existed. Even if she were legend, that wouldn't have to be terrible. It could mean there were enough people who wanted so desperately to believe this could happen, a woman could stand up and have her say, that they passed the story on for long enough that it reached me, centuries later.

"So maybe she existed," Nor says. "Maybe she didn't. Or maybe she existed, but the revenge part isn't true. There certainly would have been a lot of obstacles—"

"That's why I need it to be true!" This part is crystal clear. "I found one mention that she existed but just, like, died after the rape. That's the worst possibility. I need there to be a story—history, a precedent—where the monsters don't win. Where the girl gets revenge. Where there are actual fucking consequences."

After a long while, Nor says, "We can still have that story."

"How?"

"It doesn't matter what happened historically. I mean, I get why it matters to you. But even if she was raped and killed, you're the storyteller now. You tell whatever story you need to be true."

"But if we only tell the story we want to be true—"

"I'm not saying we ignore Marguerite's place in the world, or the fact that she was attacked, her family killed, all her obstacles. And if there were historical record, maybe it would be different. But in a case where the storyteller gets to decide which story to tell and how to tell it, maybe it's really powerful to give her an agency she didn't have in reality."

"To show her overcoming," I say.

"Right," Nor says. "Here's the thing—let's at least agree she existed. Shine some light on that. Because awesome women were erased from the narrative way more than they were invented."

"Okay."

"Then she did survive," Nor says. "She did overcome. For however long she lived, whether she ever put on armor or not, she survived. So it's your choice, but I think you should honor that by putting a fucking sword in her hand."

CONQUEROR

FOR EVERY TIME I'VE BATTLED
in my mind I'm unprepared
for the clash of steel on steel

the shriek of wounded horses
hot spray of blood upon my face
the way a person's eyes can change

one moment living organs
that have gazed upon a child, a lover,
wept tears of joy and grief

to lifeless orbs like those
we used to roll across the courtyard
in games of Conqueror.

THE SKIRMISH FINDS US
well before Autun
and though we are
the greater army
we are unprepared.

Not only I but
battle-hardened men
go into panic.

Not Zahra.
She takes one moment
to grab my hand.

For Helene.

Then she is in the fray.

MINUIT WHINNIES HIS DISMAY.
Hooves thunder all around
and someone on horseback
grabs my arm—to throw me down
I think, but it is Ismidon.

Remove your helmet!

He shouts to be heard.

They will see your sex
and you'll be spared!

They might be loath
to run me through with steel
but would not hesitate
to eviscerate me in other ways.

I shake him off
and follow my sister.

CODES OF CONDUCT DISINTEGRATE
on the field of battle.
Lessons learned at Father's side
are toddler's scribbles and this

illuminated manuscript
writ in blood.

Men lunge and thrust,
run one another through.
A man before me howls,
his eyes gouged out

vomit

blood

shit

mud

panic

sweat

entrails

Zahra dismounts and fends off
two attackers, swords flashing.
She holds her own
but not for long.

We came for Helene.
Now I fight for Zahra.

TOGETHER
they have more muscle
but Zahra and I have
fury and sisterhood.

No room for fear,
awareness of the horror
all around.
There is only

        thrust and block
        steel on steel
        anticipate
        and hope.

My sword
makes contact
not with armor
nor chain maille
but only flesh
could have that give
that shock that travels
from my victim
through my sword
and back again.

He drops his weapon
staggers back
grips his arm
where I sliced
through brigandine,
blood flowing freely.

I could end him now.
Straight through the gut
in and up, twist the blade.
Or slice the neck
if I can stand the spray
across my chest.

But I saved my sister.
It is enough.
I let him stagger away.

ONE MAN ROUTED,
Zahra and I
subdue the other.
We leave him
on the ground
alive and crying
for his mother.

There are no
mothers here.

THIS ISN'T
what I hoped for.

Obscene
that I could hope
for anything
resembling
this.

CHAPTER FORTY-TWO

I wake to a silent house, pitch-black outside.

My neck is screaming, probably because I fell asleep with a history of the Hundred Years' War for a pillow. I'm ravenous, a hunger I haven't felt in weeks.

There's a note on the ground, slipped under the door, Papi's slanting handwriting. The funny little smiley face he adds to all notes.

Hay caldo de res en la refri. Te amo.

I find the beef stew and heat it up. Sitting in the dark, I eat alone. Except I'm not. Papi is with me in every bite.

Before stumbling back to bed, I add onto his note, make my own goofy little face, and leave it on the table.

Gracias, Papi. Te amo también.

I must get Zahra
out of this madness.

But en route to cover
I see a man stumbling,
dragging a sword,
the man I thought
I'd disarmed.

He sneaks up on de Gaucourt
who'll be dead in seconds.

I shout to Zahra.

Make for the trees!

I'm right behind you!

This time
I do not let him live.

ONCE OUR WOUNDED
have been tended or
ended by misericorde

the fallen stripped of
weapons, family crests

de Gaucourt's second
leads me to a tent
alongside his. It seems
I've earned new lodgings.

You'll feast at the governor's side.

CHAPTER FORTY-THREE

When I ask Papi if he needs help with dinner the next night, he doesn't make a big deal of it. He just asks me to shred the chicken for the enchiladas while he works on the sauce.

As we move around the tiny kitchen to pull out the baking dish, grate the cheese, arrange the tortillas, it's not the choreographed dance he does with Nor. We bump into each other. I drop the cutting board. He can't find the cilantro.

But the enchiladas get made and in the oven. They smell amazing. It's comfortable in a way that feels both totally foreign and familiar. It's family.

ZAHRA AND I SINK
onto sumptuous cushions
in a tent with room
for every woman
in our party to Salette.

I remove my hauberk;
she removes hers.
Even with the outer layers
crumpled on the floor
like men left to die
we are still covered in blood.

We'll never find them.

I know.

CHAPTER FORTY-FOUR

Mom isn't home when Papi and I eat because she went to her book club. Instead of the relief I've felt each time Mom and I have avoided each other in the last week, I find myself missing her. Wishing we were all three eating this meal together.

This time I'm the one who leaves a note before retreating to my room.

Enchiladas in the fridge. Love you, Mom.

IN THE FEASTING TENT
men sit at overflowing tables,
drink as though this is a day
for celebration and not a day
of senseless slaughter.

I am led to the grandest table
to sit at de Gaucourt's side.
Zahra is swept away
by the officer who first
flipped up her visor,
who hails from Ethiopia as well.
He manages to charm despite
the smudge of blood upon his cheek.

I try and fail to catch her eye;
she laughs, a hand on his arm.

A slice of panic
shoots through me
I cannot lose Zahra
to anything, not even love.

Mademoiselle de Bressieux!

The governor began to drink
the moment the last body fell.

    My gallant savior!

Guffaws from all around
as though I did not truly
save his life.

He shoves
his second
to the side
so I may take
his seat.

    Sit! Dine!
    I would know your story.

WOULD HE THOUGH?
If I told him, might he
be forced to reflect

on every drawbridge breached
every servant, noblewoman
who looked on him in terror?

A man like him
does not achieve his rank
through basse danse
and repartee.

He will not
know my story
for I choose not to give it
but I can weave a tale
of vengeance
for my loving father
and it is not a lie.

It's simply not the truth.

CHAPTER FORTY-FIVE

I come home from writing at the library to an empty house. Mom has class tonight, so I pull last night's leftovers from the fridge.

While they're heating up, I grab a new notebook from my bag and start to look over what I wrote that day. When I hear the front door, I assume Papi's back, but it's Mom.

We've been civil for the last week, speaking to each other when necessary, only when Papi's around as a buffer.

I close the notebook. "Papi's on a job. I thought you had class."

She sets her stuff down, pulls something from her bag, and comes to sit on the barstool next to me. She sets my Moleskine notebook on the counter between us. "Student walkout to protest gun violence. Good on them. I wish I had the energy to join in, but I'm so tired."

I look at her face—really look. She's not the kind of tired a good night of sleep would fix. Or even a week at a spa. She's the tired of a woman who's been shoving her own shit down so she could keep her head above it and try to protect her daughters in a world where they never had a chance, no matter what she did.

She nods at my new notebook. It's a cheapo spiral-bound from the drugstore with some pages from the hospital notepad taped inside. Turns out words on a page don't really need a fancy, leather-bound journal. "You're still writing."

"Were you forbidding me from ever writing again?"

"Of course not. It was foolish of me to think taking this notebook would stop you from working on your story." She pushes it toward me.

"Did you . . . did you read it?"

"Sweetheart, no! I would never. Not without your permission. I promise."

Which makes me feel like shit, since I went into her stuff without her permission. Even if I had a good reason.

"You should keep writing it," she says. "If it's helping you. But . . . talk to us about it too. Or a therapist, if you want. There has to be some balance, you know?"

"What changed your mind?"

She sighs. "What you said about my own history, the teacher—"

"Mom, I'm so sorry about that, it's none of my business—"

A quick shake of her head shuts me up. "I kept waiting until you girls were old enough. I planned to tell you. But then you were old enough and I still kept putting it off. I couldn't see what use it would do. I had raised two awesome young women. Young feminists. Knowing my pain would only hurt us all.

"But it is a part of my story. And I want to tell you girls. Together. If you think Nor would want to know."

"I think she would. When you're ready."

She pats my hand, then gets up to investigate the leftovers situation.

"I'm heating up the enchiladas," I offer. "If you want some."

The surprise on her face kills me a little, but I get it. "That would be great. Thank you."

"Do you know if Jess went back to San Francisco?"

She puts water on for tea. "They did not. They're staying with Summer's parents. They feel awful about whatever happened between you two and that's all I'm authorized to say."

"Thank you for being there for them."

"Their parents are going through a lot. So Papi and I are trying to step up. I'm sorry if it's weird for you—"

"It's not. I mean, it doesn't have to be."

She nods and busies herself in the cupboard, organizing the mess of tea boxes.

"Mom, I really am so sorry. I said awful things to you. I've been a terrible friend to Jess. I really screwed up with the hashtag—"

She gives me her full attention, leaning across the counter to grab my hand. "There's no road map for this. Just because it's happened to a million women before Nor, before me, that doesn't mean anyone knows how to process it when it happens to them. You've had your own trauma in this." She gives a quick shake of her head to stop my objection. "I'm not saying it's the same; I'm saying it's valid. And yeah, you've messed some stuff up. So have I. But we keep trying. We keep loving each other. That's all we can do."

CHAPTER FORTY-SIX

It doesn't take a lot of persuasion to get Papi and Nor to help me make a medieval feast. It's not going to come close to whatever the San Francisco hipster chefs would have whipped up, and there will be no suckling pig, but we're doing our best.

We've settled on roast chicken, but it did give Papi the excuse to finally splurge on a (Goodwill) rotisserie like he's always wanted, so the bird is turning on a spit, just like in ye olden times.

Nor got here hours ago to begin the Tuscan onion confit, which has been caramelizing for ages. She stashed Mom's finished scrapbook under a pile of books on the coffee table, to be revealed later. Tonika and Wyatt showed up with a giant basket full of plums, which they'd plundered from the fruit-heavy trees near their apartment building.

Wyatt leans toward me and says, "It's not stealing if people are going to let the fruit drop to rot on the sidewalk, right?"

I sit at the kitchen table with him, pitting the plums while he chops them. Tonika's perched on a stool at the counter, following Papi's instructions for the pot pies. Nor is rolling out crust for a tart and endlessly stirring the confit.

I don't even know what confit is, but it smells amazing.

"When do Mom and Jess get here?" Nor asks from the stove.

"Depends how long it takes to get a license." I'm hoping they pass, and they'll feel like celebrating with us. With me.

Turns out it takes a while, which is good, since turns out it also takes a while to make a medieval feast. After plum chopping, Wyatt and I are on trencher duty. I have the feeling Nor has assigned us the most fool-proof tasks. But that's fine by me. I'd much rather leave her to fuss over the elderflower cream cheese tart while I flatten hunks of dough into bread plates.

By the time Mom and Jess pull up, the most amazing smells fill the house. I hurry outside so I can talk to them before they're distracted by medieval delicacies and found family.

Mom climbs out of the passenger seat and shoots me a thumbs-up.

"You passed?"

Jess gives a tiny smile I haven't seen in weeks. "Always the tone of surprise."

"They did great!" Mom gives them an awkward side hug, then starts for the house.

Jess grabs her arm and pulls her back for a proper hug. "Thank you, Kath. So much."

Mom pats their cheek. "You always have a place with us, love." She gives me a pointed look and hurries into the house.

"Is that true?" Jess looks shy, afraid I'll pounce. "I was such a jerk—"

"No, you weren't. I'm the jerk. You only told me the truth."

Jess fiddles with the cuff on their wrist. "Not necessarily. We don't know the truth."

"Exactly. We don't know." I grab the fiddly hand. "But just because I have my ideas of how to tell the story doesn't mean I can ignore yours. I want you to be a part of this. I need your voice. If you're willing."

A sly look creeps over Jess's face. "You need my doodles?"

"I am so sorry about that. Your art, your perspective—it's amazing. I think I felt like if I loosened my grip on the story at all it would fly away completely. But I don't give anything up by letting you in. I gain so much."

"You're making me blush."

"Meow."

"When you texted—"

"I was so glad you agreed to come. Now if we're good, I have a surprise for you. Are we good?"

They squeeze my hand and let me lead them up to the house, like they haven't spent most of the summer there.

"Whoa." They pause at the sound of unfamiliar voices in the kitchen, but the enticing smells draw them farther in. They stop in shock when they see their family crest, taken from sketch to wall-size banner by Tonika, who apparently makes the banners for her church and whipped this up like it was nothing.

The chosen family Jess wants, the family they deserve. I don't know if I deserve to be a part of it, but I'm going to try to earn my spot.

Family: from the Latin word for "servant."

"What is all this?" Jess asks in wonder.

Feast: from the Latin word for "joy."

"To thank you," I say. "For everything. For Marguerite. And to try to make up for the feast thing you missed."

Realization dawns and they take in the dishes spread across the counter. "You made me a medieval feast."

"I mean, you're expected to share." Tonika presents herself, introduces Wyatt, and starts showing Jess the various dishes we've made: chickpea stew with saffron, yogurt, and garlic; (stolen) plums stewed in rose water; roast chicken pot pie, intentionally free of potatoes, which hadn't made it to Europe yet, and we may be falling apart but we will be historically accurate; elderflower cream cheese tart.

We made them together.

We've gone through this whole thing together—Nor and me, Mom and Papi—picking up more family along the way. We're not all the way through it. But we keep moving forward. We keep loving each other. Serving each other.

We're not traveling alone.

THUS SHALL YOU BE

THE FEASTING OVER
we advance again.

The previous day's horrors
were but a skirmish.

Not even battle
to hardened soldiers
but I would bet
the men who died
might see it differently
if given the chance.

ZAHRA HAS A SPRING
in her step despite
the bloodstains on her tunic.

Tell me of your
handsome officer.

Color rises in her cheeks.

> *I've no idea*
> *what you mean.*

Come now.
I need
distraction.

She tells me
the things they have
in common, though
he's something like royalty
and she of lowly traders.
Perhaps, the battle over
he would take Zahra
to a land not ravaged by
one hundred years of war.

Or build a life with her
in France, where she would be
an officer's wife and no one's servant.

Either way
I cannot bear the thought
and yet it's all I want.

YOU MUST NOT COME,
I tell her
as I hoist myself
into the saddle.
Loyal Minuit.

> *Where would you*
> *have me go?*

Return to Isabella.
Wait for your officer.
See to my sister.
Be safe.

Zahra ignores me,
hoists herself
onto her steed.

> *Do not ask me to do*
> *what you cannot.*

A sharp whistle, and then:

> *De Bressieux!*

Summoned to join
de Gaucourt
at the front
of our procession,
I scowl at Zahra.

This isn't over.

MILES LATER
I muster
the courage
to ask the question
that fuels me.

Will we
meet Chalon
on the battlefield?

De Gaucourt laughs.

> *The man himself?*
> *Not likely.*
> *He is the sort of general*
> *who sends his soldiers*
> *into battle, then holds back*
> *until the battle's won.*
> *He hasn't stayed alive*
> *this long by skill.*

Perhaps Zahra and I
should both turn back.

I've put her life
in danger
every moment
since I pulled her
from that closet.

If her handsome officer
could be convinced
to take her as a bride—

but then I'm treating her
as though she's mine to give.
I cannot compel her stay or go.

I lag behind de Gaucourt
until Zahra catches up.

Her only words:

I'm staying.

We make camp
across the river
from Chalon's troops.
We'll attack at early light.

De Gaucourt has no further time
for the novelty of his lady knight;
he spends the evening
cloistered in his tent.

I spend it with Zahra
and praying to the god
of my childhood, the god
of these many wars.

Will vengeance
heal these wounds
rebuild the ruins of my life?
I realize now it won't.

That doesn't mean
it's pointless.
I have Zahra
and we are here
united in a purpose.

My first, my only thought:
                    my sisters.

If we fight, it's not
for vengeance, not to bring
the Prince of Orange down
or prove a thing to men
who think us weak
because we bleed.

If we fight, we show
each other that we're strong,
remind each other
that our blood
is stuff of life,
that we have been broken
and also rebuilt
through our love for each other,
our refusal to curl up and die.

A woman broken, rebuilt,
can conquer any sword.

I UNFOLD
the cloth,
my sister's work of art
filled with her rage
but also:

her hope.

Fine, even stitches,
the sort done
by a noble girl
who stitches not
for function but for form.

So ladylike, stitchery.
A pastime for quiet contemplation,
sitting with one's head bowed
lips sealed, knees closed.

But the fury
roiling within
as Helene's needle
pierced the cloth
produced a lance
spearing an orange.

Ainsi tu seras.

Thus shall you be.

MORNING LIGHT.
Armor on.

Ismidon tries
one more time:

> *You could wait*
> *the battle out.*
> *I'll fight for you.*

I do not need
his chivalry.

Zahra holds
hushed conversation
with her officer
and then

returns to join me
always at my side.

> *For Helene?*

FOR HELENE.
For Zahra.
For my mother
and every woman
left bleeding
on the stones,
their blood
the stuff of life until death,
for Isabella, the baby inside her.

For Helene.

The battle cry.

We fight.

RESOURCES

Among the organizations dedicated to helping survivors of sexual violence are the National Sexual Violence Resource Center (www.nsvrc.org) and the Rape, Abuse, and Incest National Network, known as RAINN (www.rainn.org). These organizations also have resources for the families and loved ones of survivors.

If you would like to speak confidentially with someone trained to hear your story, you can call 800-656-HOPE (4673).

We are in this fight together.

ACKNOWLEDGMENTS

Writing a book about—among other things—the process of writing a book is an illuminating experience. (That's it, the one illumination joke, I promise.) What I had that Em did not was an extraordinary editor journeying with me at every stage. My endless gratitude to Andrew Karre, who is the very best at what he does.

Also in my corner, my incomparable agent, Jim McCarthy—sort of my Jess, with less swordplay and more contracts. But the same amount of reality checks, talking me down from panic, and making me laugh.

Maia Kobabe's extraordinary illuminations exceeded all possible hopes and perfectly brought Jess's collaboration to life. I am so grateful for eir willingness to join me on this journey.

This book would not exist without the dedicated work of Julie Strauss-Gabel, Natalie Vielkind, Melissa Faulner, Anne Heausler, Anna Booth, Rob Farren, Jennifer Dee, Theresa Evangelista, Dana Li, and everyone at Penguin Young Readers who pours their heart into getting books into the hands of readers, especially the unparalleled School & Library team—thank you thank you thank you to Rachel, Venessa, Trevor, Carmela, and Summer. And special shout-out to my local regional sales rep, Colleen Conway!

The spark of this book was struck when Mackenzi Lee retweeted a post from Jason Porath about Marguerite de Bressieux. Thank you both for bringing her into my life.

Katie Henry, Katharine Manning, Elle Jauffret, Faith Waggoner, and Ray Stoeve gave me valuable input on all things Catholicism, legal system, and nonbinary identity. Any mistakes are my own.

I could not navigate this business without the people who started as my "writing friends" and whom now I call simply friends, including Jessica Lawson, Sharon Roat, Rajani LaRocca, Rachel Lynn Solomon, and Brent Taylor. Thank you for always being there.

All the booksellers, teachers, librarians, bloggers, bookstagrammers, and readers who supported my first novel, *Blood Water Paint*: This book would not exist without your love for Artemisia. Thank you for coming along with me again. Keep painting the blood.

And finally, my family, who referred to this book as *Lady Knight* throughout the years of its process and will probably keep calling it that because the actual title is so long, thank you for always letting me complain about publishing stuff for at least fifteen seconds before you start singing "Hard to Be the Bard" from *Something Rotten*. I love you.